"Thanks, I...
big-time fo...

She laughed. "Don't think I won't collect someday."

He shifted his weight, and she realized suddenly how close they stood.

"You can collect any time," he said, his voice a little lower now, his gaze locked with hers. His smile deepened at the corners, and her heart sped a little faster. Seth was a nice enough looking guy, but when he smiled…like this…wow.

Still looking into her eyes, he lowered his head a little more. Very slowly, giving her plenty of time to draw back or turn her cheek if she wanted. She tilted her face upward instead.

His lips brushed hers lightly. It was a friendly kiss, neither demanding nor tentative. Yet when it ended and he drew back to smile at her again, she felt very much as if they'd just stepped over an invisible line between friendly neighbors and something a little more…intimate.

Dear Reader,

I was recently asked if I have a recurring "theme" in my writing. So many of my books are set in series about close-knit families. The question made me ponder what family means to me. Security? Companionship? Validation? The theme I finally selected was Sanctuary. Family, to me, is a safe place to take refuge from an unpredictable, sometimes scary world. A place to find reassurance and acceptance—not idyllic or conflict-free, but filled with love. I've been blessed that this has always been my experience with family—the one I was born into, the one I married into and the one my husband and I created together during the past thirty plus years.

In this new series, Doctors in the Family, you'll meet three siblings who all happen to be doctors, but who face many of the same family issues as those in any profession. Too many responsibilities, too little time, worrisome illnesses, loss of loved ones, stepparenting and adapting to the inevitable changes that come with passing time. And always love. I hope you enjoy reading about Meagan, Mitch and Madison—and the families they encounter in their stories!

Visit me any time at ginawilkins.com.

Gina Wilkins

THE M.D.
NEXT DOOR

GINA WILKINS

SPECIAL EDITION®

Published by Silhouette Books

America's Publisher of Contemporary Romance

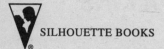 SILHOUETTE BOOKS

Recycling programs
for this product may
not exist in your area.

ISBN-13: 978-0-373-65574-8

THE M.D. NEXT DOOR

Books by Gina Wilkins

Silhouette Special Edition

***The Stranger in Room 205* #1399
***Bachelor Cop Finally Caught?* #1413
***Dateline Matrimony* #1424
The Groom's Stand-In #1460
The Best Man's Plan #1479
*The Family Plan #1525
**Conflict of Interest* #1531
‡*Faith, Hope and Family* #1538
Make-Believe Mistletoe #1583
Countdown to Baby #1592
The Homecoming #1652
‡*Adding to the Family* #1712
‡*The Borrowed Ring* #1717
‡*The Road to Reunion* #1735
The Date Next Door #1799
The Bridesmaid's Gifts #1809
Finding Family #1892
The Man Next Door #1905
The Texan's Tennessee Romance #1954
††*Diagnosis: Daddy* #1990
††*Private Partners* #2027
††*The Doctor's Undoing* #2057
††*Prognosis: Romance* #2069
†*The M.D. Next Door* #2092

Silhouette Books

Mother's Day Collection 1995
Three Mothers and a Cradle
"Beginnings"

World's Most Eligible Bachelors
Doctor in Disguise

Logan's Legacy
The Secret Heir

‡Family Found
**Hot Off the Press
*The McClouds of Mississippi
††Doctors in Training
†Doctors in the Family

GINA WILKINS

is a bestselling and award-winning author who has written more than seventy novels for Harlequin and Silhouette Books. She credits her successful career in romance to her long, happy marriage and her three "extraordinary" children.

A lifelong resident of central Arkansas, Ms. Wilkins sold her first book to Harlequin in 1987 and has been writing full-time since. She has appeared on the Waldenbooks, B. Dalton and *USA TODAY* bestseller lists. She is a three-time recipient of the Maggie Award for Excellence, sponsored by Georgia Romance Writers, and has won several awards from the reviewers of *RT Book Reviews*.

For my wonderful family, near and far.

Chapter One

Dressed in a long-sleeved purple T-shirt and comfort-able black yoga pants, Meagan Baker reclined in a padded chaise lounge. She had a white cashmere shawl draped over her shoulders, cold soda by her hand, good book in her lap. The chair was one of several arranged in a com-panionable grouping on the rock patio surrounding her smallish, in-ground pool, which sparkled in the afternoon sun. A spreading oak tree canopied with early spring leaves shaded her chair. Birds played among the branches, sing-ing cheerily. A pleasant, floral-fragrant breeze brushed her cheeks and rustled the new leaves above her, harmonizing sweetly with the birdsongs.

Glumly, she studied her feet clad in flirty purple ballet flats. Most people would think she was crazy for wishing she were in an operating room in scrubs, paper gown, cap and mask, and arch-supporting shoes.

"Can I get you anything else, sweetie?"

She forced a smile as she looked up at her mother, who hovered nearby. "I'm fine, thanks. You should go home and take care of Meemaw."

"You're sure?" Her mom, LaDonna Baker, looked torn between caring for her convalescing daughter and returning home to tend to her own ailing mother, who lived with her. "I could warm a pot of soup before I go."

"I can warm my own soup. You've filled my fridge and freezer with meals I can pop into the microwave. I won't go hungry." Meagan hated the feeling that she was adding to her mother's already sizeable load of responsibilities. As the eldest of three children and a surgeon by trade, Meagan was much more accustomed to being a caretaker than having one.

Only a couple of days out of the hospital after undergoing emergency surgery, she still felt annoyingly weak and achy. She had pain pills if she needed them, but she limited herself to over-the-counter meds as much as possible. Having declined an invitation to recuperate at her mother's house, Meagan preferred to keep her head clear. She lived alone, but she had promised her concerned family she would keep a cell phone always close at hand. Her mother and two physician siblings all lived within a ten-minute drive, so she had no fears about being on her own.

"Go home, Mom," she repeated gently. "You've been here most of the day. I know you have things to do at home."

Torn by her responsibilities, her mother finally, reluctantly left, though she made Meagan promise to call if she needed anything. Anything at all.

Alone at last, Meagan rested her head against the back of her chair and closed her eyes. She hadn't wanted to display her weakness in front of her worried mother, but now she could relax and moan, unheard by anyone but herself.

She remembered patients complaining they felt as though they'd been hit by a truck; she now knew exactly what they meant. Every inch of her seemed to ache or throb, not just the healing incision in her abdomen. She'd always tried to be sympathetic to her patients' discomfort, but she thought she'd be even more so now that she'd actually experienced post-surgical pain, herself.

As much as she appreciated her mother's loving care, it felt good to be alone for a while and outside in the fresh air. Ever since she'd been hospitalized six days ago for emergency surgery to repair an ovarian torsion, she'd been pent up and poked at and hovered over and treated like a… well, like a patient. She had quickly realized that she much preferred being the doctor.

She rested a hand lightly on the incision site, from force of habit, feeling for excessive heat or swelling. Despite her discomfort, she was healing just fine. She wished fleetingly that the surgery could have been performed laparoscopically, which would have resulted in a much shorter recovery period, but her condition had been too severe. Her left ovary had been twisted to the point of necrosis, and the surgeon had been unable to salvage it.

She might have saved the ovary if she'd caught the condition earlier, Meagan thought regretfully. She had mistaken the symptomatic pain for her usual menstrual cramping, popping OTC pain relievers and staying too busy taking care of other people to pay attention to her own well-being—a common failing among physicians. Only when she'd been incapacitated by sudden, severe pain, nausea and fever had she sought emergency care. She'd been rushed into an O.R. by a surgeon she worked with and trusted implicitly. If anyone could have salvaged the ovary, it would have been Meilin Liu, but no such luck.

It still surprised her how shaken she had been by the

crisis. Meagan had spent the past ten years in the medical field, but seeing it from a hospital bed had been a completely different experience. She had been fortunate not to have had any health crises during her first thirty-two years, having been hospitalized only once for a tonsillectomy when she was nine. She had decided then that she wanted to be a doctor, but she had been so young she hardly remembered the hospital experience itself.

This had been different. She'd been forced during the past week to face both her mortality and her fertility, and she had been taken aback by her reactions.

Meilin had assured her the loss of an ovary would not prevent her from conceiving a child. But Meagan was thirty-two and not even dating anyone in particular. She had maybe another decade, more or less, to have a child should she decide to do so.

As for mortality—she had always thought there would be plenty of time for the things she had neglected in her single-minded pursuit of her career. Hobbies. Travel. Marriage. Children. Now she was suddenly aware of how quickly time had passed. Her twenties had sped by in a blur of medical school studying, long, sleepless residency hours, then establishing her practice as a surgeon in a Little Rock, Arkansas teaching hospital. The people she loved were growing older. Her mother was nearing sixty, her grandmother was in her eighties. Her younger brother had just turned thirty and their little sister wasn't far behind.

She remembered as a child hearing older people talk about how quickly time flew. Back then she hadn't understood; now she identified all too well with that sentiment.

"Oof!" Her wistful musings ended abruptly when a solid, wiggling weight landed directly on her stomach, only inches from her still-healing incision.

"What the—?"

Warm breath bathed her face while an eager pink tongue tried to do the same. Her hands were filled with a squirming, panting yellow puppy—a good-sized one at that, with paws as big as her fists and a smiling, wet-nosed face. The dog wasn't still long enough for her to read the red metal tag dangling from his collar. Every time one of his big feet landed on her abdomen, she groaned.

"Waldo!"

A girl with a fresh, freckled face almost hidden behind round glasses and an unruly mop of brown curls rushed to rescue Meagan from the friendly assault. She grabbed the pup and wrestled him into a firm clench in her skinny arms. "Be still, Waldo. I'm so sorry, ma'am. I hope he didn't scare you. He's really friendly."

Apparently, Meagan's mom had accidentally left the backyard gate open when she left. Pressing one hand to her throbbing scar and wiping her damp cheek with the other, Meagan managed to smile at the girl. "He is definitely friendly. You called him Waldo?"

The girl nodded shyly. "My dad named him that because we're always asking where's Waldo?"

Meagan laughed, which only made her incision hurt worse. "Cute. You'd better keep him on a leash, though. I'd hate for him to run out in the street and get hit."

"He got away from me when I was trying to untangle his leash." Juggling the dog, the girl managed to snap a sturdy leather leash onto his collar. Only then did she set him down, clinging to the strap with both hands when he immediately tried to dash away from her. He almost tugged her off her feet before she braced herself. "Be still, Waldo. We're taking him to obedience classes."

Meagan eyed the bounding pup skeptically. "Um—how's that going?"

"We just signed him up for six classes. They start a week from Saturday."

The dog pounced on the only errant dandelion sprouting from Meagan's immaculate backyard and enthusiastically ripped the puff from the top, shaking his head, play-growling and scattering seeds everywhere. Meagan thought the obedience class teacher would have quite a challenge with this particular student.

"I'm Alice Llewellyn," the girl volunteered, still clinging to the leash. "I live in the red brick house on the other side of the street, two houses down."

Though she had never met the inhabitants, Meagan knew the house. She nodded. "Hi, Alice. I'm Meagan Baker."

"We just moved here a couple of weeks ago. I haven't met many of the neighbors yet."

Meagan had lived in this upscale, young-professionals neighborhood for almost two years and hadn't met many of her neighbors either. It wasn't that she was unfriendly, she assured herself. She simply wasn't home much. Her working hours started very early, so she rarely saw any neighbors when headed for the hospital. She usually returned home tired and hungry, drove straight into the garage and put the door down behind her, then walked directly into her kitchen. Because of her busy schedule, she paid someone to keep up her lawn and pool. She did her walking and weight training at the hospital gym. And while she enjoyed swimming laps in her solar-heated pool, she usually did so after dark within the privacy of her tall redwood fence— the gate of which was now swinging open.

"It's very nice to meet you, Alice. Welcome to the neighborhood."

The dandelion conquered and demolished, Waldo moved on to sniff the base of an azalea bush covered in pink blooms. Fortunately Alice tugged him away from it before he could destroy that, too.

"When we moved here, I hoped there would be some other kids my age in one of the houses close to ours," Alice confided. "My best friends from school live in other parts of town, so someone has to drive me to their houses. We're on spring break from school, but there aren't any other teenagers to hang out with on this street. A few little kids, but no one my age. I turned thirteen last week."

Alice was quite obviously proud to call herself a teenager now, Meagan thought with a smothered smile. "Happy belated birthday."

Alice grinned, showing a quick flash of braces. "Thanks. Waldo was my birthday present. But now my dad says he wishes he'd bought me something less destructive. Like a chainsaw."

Alice's dad seemed to have quite the sense of humor. Because the girl seemed lonely, Meagan motioned toward another outdoor chair. "Would you like to have a seat? I can get you a soda or some lemonade."

"No, thank you, my nan—um, the housekeeper is probably wondering where I am."

Meagan deliberately gave no indication that she'd noticed the young teen's quick substitute of the word housekeeper for nanny. Teenagers, of course, would never admit to having or needing a nanny.

"I like your pool," Alice added with a glance around the backyard. "Dad says maybe we'll get one when he gets time to think about it. He's a lawyer and he's been real busy at work lately. There was a pool at the condo where he used to live, but he decided he needed a real house now that I live with him and this one didn't come with a pool. It has room for one in the backyard, though, so he said he'll think about it because I love to swim."

Charmed by the artless chatter, even though she was bemused by how much personal information the girl had crammed into a few sentences, Meagan motioned toward her small, but functional pool. "You'd be welcome to swim in mine during your spring break. I'm home every day for the next few weeks to recover from a surgical procedure, and I'd enjoy the company if it's okay with your dad and your, um, housekeeper. The pool is heated, so you'd be warm enough as long as you bring a cover-up for when you get out of the water. As warm as it has been this month, it's still a little too cool to stand around in a wet bathing suit."

Alice's face lit up with her smile, making Meagan realize the girl was actually quite pretty beneath the glasses and wild hair. "That would be so cool. I really love to swim. I'll ask my dad. I'm sure he'll say it's okay. Thanks, Miss Baker."

"You can just call me Meagan." She'd never been one to insist on being called "doctor," like some of her more pretentious colleagues.

"Thanks, Meagan. I'll see you later, okay? Come on, Waldo, let's go home."

"Would you mind closing the gate behind you?"

"Sure. See you later."

Meagan watched in amusement as Alice tugged at the leash to get the rambunctious pup headed in the right direction, then was nearly pulled off her feet when the dog dashed away. Obedience classes were definitely going to be interesting with Waldo in them.

"So then Waldo took a big jump right into the pool. Water sprayed everywhere and he yelped like he was surprised he got wet. Then he started swimming and splashing and shaking his ears and he had the best time. Me and Meagan—"

"Meagan and I."

Setting a plate on the dining room table for Friday evening's dinner, Alice continued with barely a pause for her father's correction. "Meagan and I were laughing so hard at him, and that just made him act sillier. She said she didn't mind letting him into her pool because she has someone who cleans it for her. Waldo loves going swimming, Dad. We really should get a pool."

"If we get a pool," Seth Llewellyn replied firmly, laying napkins beside the two place settings on their table, "it will be for our use, not for Waldo's."

Alice gave him an innocent look. "Of course. But we can let Waldo swim with us, too, can't we?"

"We'll see how he does in obedience classes."

"He'll ace them, you'll see," Alice said confidently. "He's really very intelligent."

Seth was still reserving judgment on that call.

At least they could eat in peace. The rowdy dog was safe in the fenced backyard. He had a cozy, overpriced dog house to keep him warm and dry, and more toys than any one dog should own. Within the course of the past ten days, Waldo had gone from shelter pup to pampered pet and he was adjusting quite happily to the transition.

When Seth had taken Alice to the Humane Society to rescue a dog for her birthday present, he'd given her the choice of adopting a small, indoor dog or a larger dog that would live outside. She'd chosen the latter, though she'd hinted broadly that one of the homeless cats in the shelter would do quite well inside their house. Seth had told her hastily that they would concentrate on one pet at a time for now.

"Meagan said she thinks Waldo will be the greatest

dog ever once he graduates from obedience school." Alice shook out her napkin and laid it across her lap without pausing to breathe. "She thinks he'll be sitting and staying by the end of the first lesson and heeling and fetching by the third. Maybe I can even teach him some fun tricks—you know, like roll over and play dead and..."

"And wash the dishes and take out the trash and scrub the toilets."

Alice laughed musically. "Daddy, he's just a dog."

"Mmm. Tell your friend Meagan that."

"She knows. She calls him my wild child now, but she says she's being an optimist about obedience classes."

Seth had yet to catch a glimpse of his daughter's new friend, though Nina, the sixty-two-year-old housekeeper who doubled as a caretaker for his young daughter, had discreetly checked her out. When Alice had asked permission to go swimming at the neighbor's house during her spring break, he'd agreed only on the condition that Nina would first meet the woman and confirm that Alice was a welcome guest. Nina had reported back that there was no reason for concern about the situation.

Nina had apparently liked Meagan Baker immediately. She had confirmed Alice's explanation that the woman was home from work on a medical leave and seemed to enjoy Alice's company during the afternoons. Neither Alice nor Nina had mentioned what Meagan did for a living, though Alice had said vaguely that she believed Meagan worked at the local teaching hospital. Seth had formed a hazy image of a middle-aged secretary or insurance clerk recuperating from a hysterectomy or some such female ailment.

Alice was certainly taken with Meagan. During the past three days, all Seth had heard from her during the dinners they shared was "Meagan said this" and "Meagan said that."

He was aware that Alice missed her mother. His ex-wife had moved to Hong Kong six months ago to accept an impressive position with an American law firm there. Though she called Alice almost every day, the distance between them was hard on them. Seth knew how Colleen had agonized before accepting that job she had wanted so desperately. Her long hours and freely acknowledged ambition had ruled out Alice joining her there, even if Seth would have agreed—which he would not have, not without a battle.

Though he, too, was an attorney with a busy schedule, Seth had always been the one to scale back his hours to allow time for Alice even if he risked forfeiting career advancements at times. He and Colleen had shared custody while Colleen lived in the same country, but Seth had always been the primary caregiver. Colleen loved their daughter as much as he did, but ambition had always come first for her.

She would be the first to admit that family had been sacrificed on the altar of career in her case, ending their ill-fated marriage and affecting her relationship with her only child. More than once Colleen had confessed to Seth that she simply wasn't the maternal type. Had she not accidentally become pregnant with Alice while she and Seth were dating in law school, she probably would never have had a child. There would be no others for her.

They'd both been twenty-three and in their first year of law school when Alice was conceived in a spontaneous interlude during what was to have been a study session. After taking a couple of weeks to consider her options, Colleen had suggested it was actually the ideal time to start a family, before they graduated and leapt into the race for career advancement. She'd been a bit concerned that having a child would be counted against her in job interviews, but there was always the appearance of settled respectability to balance that, she'd concluded. If she could demonstrate that she could graduate at the top of her class after pregnancy and childbirth, then she could surely convince any potential employers that she was prepared for all challenges.

Encouraged by their youthful infatuation and confident determination, they had married, thinking they had enough in common to sustain a long-term partnership. They were both fascinated by the law, though Seth's interests ran to local corporate practice while Colleen's sights had been set on more far-reaching and international goals. They got along well, and were great together in bed. Both came from successful, overachieving families and would be able to afford housekeepers and nannies to help them run their household. They figured marriage and parenthood would be easy compared to their other achievements.

Their common grounds had not been enough to overcome the other obstacles between them. The divorce had been reasonably amicable, the division of property and terms of custody settled with only a few heated battles in the process. The past six years had passed quickly and relatively quietly. Seth had risen into a junior partnership at a prestigious Little Rock law firm while Colleen traveled extensively in her skyrocketing international law career, leaving Alice more and more in Seth's care. He and Colleen had remained on distantly friendly terms. After all, they would be bound for the rest of their lives by the daughter they both loved, so they might as well make it as pleasant as possible for everyone involved.

Was Alice subconsciously searching for another female role model in her new friendship with Meagan, or was she simply a bit lonely in her new neighborhood and looking for entertainment? With an all-too-familiar pinch of parental guilt, Seth wondered if he should have done more to provide activities for her during this week off. He'd thought spending time with her new puppy and her beloved books and art supplies would have kept her entertained for a few days out of classes.

Unfortunately, he was involved in an important and convoluted case with one of his most influential clients and it simply hadn't been possible for him to get away from work now. He'd have to work quite a bit this weekend, too, but the case should be resolved by the middle of next week. There would be other cases, of course, and piles of other career responsibilities but he was going to take his full two weeks of vacation this summer to spend with Alice, whatever it took to accomplish that feat.

He'd have a whole month this summer—the last two weeks of June and the first two weeks of July—to devote to clearing his schedule. Alice would be spending those four weeks in Europe with her mother, who was combining some vacation time with a few business obligations in France, Switzerland and Belgium. Colleen had arranged her schedule so Alice would join her in London, then accompany her on her travels during the following month, along with a responsible au pair to entertain Alice when Colleen was busy.

Seth dreaded those weeks. He would miss Alice horribly. He would also worry about her safety the entire time, though he knew Colleen would be as obsessively conscientious about that as she was with all the other details in her minutely-organized life.

"This dinner looks good," he said, slicing into the chicken enchilada on his plate. "I'm starving."

Alice smiled smugly. "I helped Nina make the enchiladas. She's teaching me to cook. And she's going to teach me to knit. We were talking while we made the enchiladas and I said I wished I knew how to knit and she said she used to knit all the time before her arthritis made it hard for her to hold the needles for too long, but she said she was sure she could teach me if I really want to learn. She's bringing needles and yarn Monday. Cool, huh?"

"Very cool." He loved that his daughter had an almost insatiable thirst for knowledge. She wanted to learn about everything. She'd been taking piano lessons since she was eight, and played clarinet in school band. She was an avid reader and enjoyed visiting museums and science exhibits. Yet he made sure she took some time just to relax and play, something neither he nor Colleen had been encouraged to do as children.

Seth's father was still a workaholic architect and his late mother had worked for the state government in a high-pressure, supervisory position in the family services department. His mother had dropped dead at fifty-one of a massive heart attack; she'd been in the middle of a conference call when it had happened. That had been ten years ago. Seth had vowed then that he wouldn't let his job work him to death.

Playtime and vacations had been very rare in his own overly scheduled and often-lonely childhood; he had tried very hard to make Alice's different despite his career obligations. And if there were times when he felt like he neglected his own needs in favor of hers and his job's—well, that was a choice he'd made when he'd become a single dad. All too soon, she would be eighteen and leaving for college. He'd have plenty of time for himself then, he thought with a ripple of anticipatory melancholy.

He had just swallowed his first spicy bite of chicken enchilada when the doorbell rang. With a frown, he set down his fork. He wasn't expecting company. It was a little late for deliveries. Casting a wistful glance at his cooling meal, he rose. "I'll be right back."

Anxious to get back to his dinner, he opened the front door without checking to see who stood on the other side. He blinked a few times when he recognized Waldo, wiggling and yapping like the idiot mutt he was. And then his gaze lifted to the face of the slender blonde woman awkwardly juggling the squirming pup in her arms.

"Are you missing someone?" she asked in a pleasant, amused voice.

The dog barked happily, twisting his head to lick his companion's chin.

"Waldo!" Having heard the commotion, Alice rushed forward to rescue the caller from the dog. "How did you get out?"

"He came to my door," the woman explained, rather eagerly surrendering her burden. "I heard scratching and when I went to investigate, he bounded right inside as if he'd come for dinner. I told him he was out of luck because I haven't cooked anything yet. I figured you didn't know he was out."

"No, we didn't." Seth glanced at Alice. "Obviously he's found a break somewhere in the fence. He'll have to stay in the garage until I can find where he got out. I'll look as soon as we've finished eating."

"Bad boy, Waldo," Alice scolded. "You could have been hit by a car! You're just lucky Meagan rescued you before you got hurt."

"Put him in the garage and wash your hands, Alice. We'll take care of him after dinner." He knew they would never be able to eat in peace if they left the boisterous pup in the house. He certainly hoped the obedience classes would be as worthwhile as Alice predicted.

He turned back to their caller when Alice hauled the dog away. "Thanks for bringing him home. I guess."

She smiled. "You're welcome. You're Alice's dad?"

"Yes, I'm Seth Llewellyn. And you must be Meagan Baker. Alice talks about you all the time."

Alice hadn't mentioned, though, that their neighbor was in her early thirties and quite attractive. Her just-above-shoulder-length hair looked soft and slightly wavy, probably salon-lightened to a pretty honey blond. Her eyes were blue, her gaze direct and confident. She didn't appear to be wearing much makeup, but then she didn't need any. Her skin was smooth and clear, a little pale, and her nicely-shaped mouth was a soft, natural pink. Very nice.

They shook hands, and he noticed her grip was firm, her skin smooth and warm.

"Alice is such a sweet girl. I've enjoyed visiting with her." She smiled as she spoke, making him believe her.

"She enjoyed spending time with you this week." He grimaced ruefully. "I wish I could have spent more time with her during her break but I couldn't get away from work. I hoped her new pup would entertain her for a few days, but having you to visit and being able to swim in your pool has really added to her enjoyment of the days off from school."

"I'm glad. She's made my week pass more quickly, too. I'm not used to being at home with nothing much to do."

Seth studied her face more closely. Her skin was naturally fair, but was she just a bit too pale?

"Are you okay?" he asked tentatively. "You look a little—"

She pushed a strand of hair from her face and he noted her hand wasn't quite steady.

"I had surgery two weeks ago," she admitted, and he thought he detected just a hint of frustration in her tone. "I guess Waldo was a little heavier than I realized."

He recalled that he'd been ordered not to lift anything heavy for a few weeks after an emergency appendectomy back in college, the only time he'd had surgery. Waldo was not only rather heavy, he'd probably wiggled and squirmed all the way from Meagan's house.

"You should have called us to come get him. Please, come in and sit down for a minute. Let me get you a glass of water."

"I didn't have your number. And I'll be fine, really. I don't want to disturb your dinner."

"You said you haven't made anything for yourself yet. Why don't you join us? There's plenty of food."

Returning just in time to hear the offer, Alice added her own appeal. "Oh, yes, join us, Meagan. We just started eating. I helped Nina cook, and she said we made way too much for just two people."

Looking a little flustered, Meagan demurred at first, but Alice was hard to resist. Mere minutes later, the three of them sat at the dining table where Alice served Meagan a heaping plate of chicken enchiladas and Spanish rice while Seth poured their guest a glass of raspberry iced tea.

She seemed to be catching her breath, he noted in satisfaction as she sipped the tea. Her cheeks were a healthy pink now, and the faint lines of pain around her mouth had eased. It had been very thoughtful of her to return Alice's fugitive mutt despite the discomfort it had caused her.

They didn't have to worry about making conversation. Alice took care of that for them, chattering almost without stopping while they ate. She told them all the latest news from her school friends, gleaned from phone calls and internet friend sites. She babbled about her hopes for Waldo's training, and all the tricks she wanted to teach him once he'd mastered basic obedience. She shared a funny story her mom had told her in their daily phone call about a reckless cab driver in Hong Kong.

"I'm going to Europe in June, did I tell you, Meagan?" she asked, using the anecdote as a segue.

"Yes, you've told me."

Judging from Meagan's tone, Seth suspected Alice had mentioned the upcoming trip several times, but Meagan still sounded encouraging when she added, "I know you're really looking forward to the adventure."

Alice nodded with the eagerness and trace of hesitation she always displayed when they talked about her trip. "It'll be great to be with Mom and see all those countries. But I guess I'm a little nervous about the flight to London. I've never been on a flight that long by myself before."

"You'll be fine. My younger sister Madison went to France when she wasn't much older than you to visit a school friend whose family had moved there. She was fifteen, I think, which would have made it about twelve years ago. Our parents were nervous about letting her go, but they knew it was a great opportunity for her. The flight attendants took very good care of her and escorted her straight to her hosts when they reached their destination. She had a fabulous time."

Alice seemed to find reassurance in Meagan's story. Seth tried to find some measure of encouragement, himself, though he couldn't help thinking the world had changed in those past twelve years. He dreaded the day he put Alice on that plane, though he was doing his best to keep her from seeing the extent of his reluctance.

"I didn't know you have a sister, Meagan," Alice said, already skipping to the next topic.

"I have a sister and a brother, both younger. Madison and Mitchell. My parents had a thing for the letter *M*, apparently," Meagan added with a wrinkle of her nose that Seth found enchanting.

"Are you close to them?"

The faintest hint of wistfulness in Alice's question made Seth frown. Alice had a few weapons in her arsenal for making-dad-feel-guilty. A couple of times she had pulled out the I'm-an-only-child-from-a-broken-home lament, just to see how far it would take her in an argument. She had learned quickly enough that it didn't take her far at all, but he knew he would hear versions of the grievance again.

As well behaved as she was, Alice was a normal kid just coming into the hormonal teen years. He suspected there would be conflicts ahead in which she would not hesitate to pull out whatever tool she deemed most useful for manipulating Dad. He'd been warned about it by several friends and coworkers with teenagers, and he thought he was as prepared as he could possibly be. At least, he hoped so, he thought with a swallow.

"I am close to my siblings," Meagan replied lightly. "As much as we can be, at least, with all of us so busy in our careers. We try to get together at least once a month and to call each other several times a week. Our mom is the one who keeps us all informed about what's going on with the others."

"We don't have a big family," Alice confided. "Dad's an only child and his mom died when I was too little to remember her. Grampa Llewellyn lives in Dallas, and we only see him a few times a year. My mom has a sister who lives in Denver. She has two kids, but they're older than me and I don't know them very well. I see my mom's parents, though. They live in Heber Springs and I spend one weekend a month with them."

Seth wondered what it was about Meagan that turned his normally somewhat-reserved-with-outsiders daughter into such a chatterbox. Even if Alice were looking for someone to fill in for her absent mother, Meagan bore little resemblance to Colleen, either physically or in mannerisms.

Colleen's appearance was a bit more striking than Meagan's, a slightly exotic attractiveness she played up deliberately with makeup and fashions. Meagan was more girl-next-door pretty, a look he found more appealing these days. Colleen spoke in a mile-a-minute, no-nonsense tone, all traces of the South deliberately scrubbed from her accent. Meagan's voice was softer, her speech slower, the slight hint of Southern drawl soothing and charming, in his opinion.

Both women projected intelligence, competence and independence—at least, from what little he'd seen of Meagan—but Mcagan was less...well, stressful was the first word that popped into his mind. Maybe Alice focused more on the few qualities her mother and her neighbor shared rather than the differences. Or maybe she just enjoyed having the attention of any encouraging adult, he thought with another little ripple of guilt.

He could sort of understand Alice's fascination. As the meal progressed, he realized he wouldn't mind having Meagan Baker's attention, himself. Granted, it had been a while since he'd spent an intimate evening with an attractive woman, considering how busy he'd been with work and his daughter. But he thought it was more than that, that drew him to his appealing neighbor. Maybe he was falling under the same spell that seemed to have affected his daughter.

He wasn't sure whether to be more intrigued or unnerved by the possibility.

"Did you hear me, Dad?" Alice asked with an exasperation that made him suspect he'd momentarily tuned her out.

"Sorry, Roo, I was concentrating on this delicious dinner you prepared. What were you saying?"

She rolled her eyes in response to both the childhood

nickname and the blatant flattery. "I said I need you to take me shopping tomorrow. You know, for the class party tomorrow night? I tried on the dress I was planning to wear—the really pretty one Mom bought me before she left for Hong Kong—and it's gotten too little. I guess I've grown a little taller in the past six months."

He heard both pride and disappointment in her tone. She'd worried about being a "late bloomer," shorter and less developed than some of her classmates, and he suspected she was relieved by the recent growth spurt but he knew she'd wanted to wear that fancy dress. She'd worn it only once, at a Christmas party with her maternal grandparents.

He'd thought when she'd first shown it to him that the expensive garment had been a frivolous purchase at her age. She didn't attend that many dressy parties, and she was growing too fast to invest too much in clothes that wouldn't fit her in another couple of months. Colleen wasn't usually so impractical, but he suspected she'd been suffering from a guilty conscience at her impending move so far from her daughter. She'd given Alice several lavish gifts before her departure.

And speaking of guilt....

"I'm sorry, Alice. I have to work tomorrow. I'll ask Nina to take you shopping in the morning."

"But, Dad."

Uh-oh. He knew this tone. "Alice—"

"Can't you take just a couple of hours in the morning before you go to the office? I'll choose fast, I promise."

Wishing fervently that she'd waited until they were alone to start this particular argument, he shook his head in regret. "I'm sorry, I can't. I have a meeting that starts at nine, before most of the shops even open. It will last most of the day, and that would be too late to find you a dress and get you to the party on time. You should have tried the dress on sooner, rather than waiting until the last minute. Surely you have something else you can wear. You went shopping with your grandmother just last month."

"We bought new school uniforms and some weekend clothes. I just won't go to the party," Alice finished with a melodramatic sigh. "I'll stay home and play with Waldo or something."

He winced in response to her long-suffering, self-pitying tone. Great. Could she make him look like a worse parent in front of her new friend? "Okay, maybe I can—"

"I'd be happy to take you shopping, Alice," Meagan volunteered unexpectedly—or had that been his daughter's hope all along? "If it's okay with your father, of course."

Finding himself the focus of two pairs of feminine eyes, Seth reached for his tea glass to wash down a bite of enchilada that seemed to have caught in his throat. How was he to say anything but yes when his daughter and their pretty neighbor were both looking at him so expectantly?

Chapter Two

Meagan couldn't help but take pity on Alice's dad. Alice had certainly put him on the spot with her last-minute plea. Now a near stranger had offered to take his daughter shopping.

Meagan knew all about work obligations, and she didn't blame Seth for not being able to change his plans on such short notice. As he'd pointed out, Alice should have tried on the dress earlier in the week. But Meagan could offer assistance this time. It wasn't as if she had anything more pressing to do, she thought with an increasingly-familiar impatience to get back to her own busy life.

"We couldn't ask you to do that," Seth protested politely. "You're still recovering from surgery."

She figured he was remembering her momentary spell of weakness after she'd delivered Waldo, and it galled her that he'd seen that. She didn't like being perceived as sickly or frail. "Chasing down Waldo and wrestling him over here was a little strenuous, but I'd be fine to watch Alice try on clothes. I'm cleared to drive now, no longer on any prescription pain meds. It would actually be good for me to get out and get some light exercise."

"We won't overdo it, Dad," Alice added eagerly. "We can go to the mall, that's not far. I'm sure I'll find a dress really fast, so we won't be gone long. I bet Meagan could help me pick the perfect outfit for the party. Please, Daddy?"

Meagan thought Seth still looked uncomfortable with the impromptu plan, but he was unable to resist his daughter's hopeful expression. "Okay, if you're sure you don't mind, Meagan. I'll give you my cell phone number. Feel free to call if you need anything, even if you have to interrupt my meeting."

"We'll be fine," Meagan assured him.

She'd never taken a teenager shopping for clothes before, but she thought it might be fun. "Maybe I'll call Madison and see if she wants to join us. She's the fashion expert in our family and I think you and she would enjoy meeting, Alice. We could have lunch at the Chinese restaurant downstairs in the mall—do you like Chinese?"

"I love Chinese!" Alice almost bounced in her seat in excitement.

Laughing, Meagan nodded. "Then we'll make it a girls' day out. I'm not sure Madison can join us. She has a very busy schedule. If she can't, we'll have fun, just the two of us."

"I'm sure we will," Alice agreed with a grin that made her braces flash in the light of the dining room chandelier.

Seth cleared his throat, and Meagan wondered if he was feeling a bit left out. "Did you and Nina make any dessert to go with this meal, Alice?"

Alice jumped out of her chair. "We made flan! I'll serve. Do you like flan, Meagan?"

"I love it," she replied honestly.

Seth rose a bit more leisurely. "I put on a pot of decaf just before we sat down to eat. Would you like a cup with your dessert, Meagan?"

"Yes, thank you."

Insisting she remain seated, he carried her plate and utensils into the kitchen with him. He was obviously handy around the house, she mused with a slight smile. She supposed that had developed from being a single dad. Alice had told her Nina worked weekdays until five and half days on Saturdays, taking care of the household duties and cooking, but Alice grumbled that she was expected to do quite a few chores, herself. Her dad, she'd said, took care of meals on Saturday evenings and Sundays. He was a pretty good cook, she'd added proudly, but sometimes they ate out when the hardworking attorney was too tired or busy to prepare meals.

Meagan had gotten the impression of a well-run, tightly scheduled household. Alice seemed generally satisfied with the routines, though perhaps a bit lonely at times. She was obviously crazy about her father, and seemed to have little resentment about her mother's absence, though Meagan had heard occasional undertones of wistfulness in the girl's voice when she'd spoken of her mom. All in all, Alice seemed to be a happy, well-adjusted girl, which spoke well of her busy father's parenting skills.

Meagan studied Seth when he returned with two cups of steaming coffee, setting one in front of her before returning to his seat. She had been a little surprised when he had opened the door to her earlier. Alice had talked about him quite a bit, of course, but Meagan's mental picture of him had been rather different from the reality. He was younger than she'd expected, for one thing. She wasn't very good at guessing age, but he looked to be thirty-five, thirty-six, maybe—which meant he'd been young when Alice was born. Definitely nice looking, with wide-set green eyes, thick, slightly wavy brown hair and a firm, faintly indented chin. Alice had gotten her coloring and facial shape from him, apparently, though her brown eyes must have come from her mother.

He seemed quite nice. Amusing, thoughtful, devoted to his daughter. The latter quality was the one that precluded him from being someone she might have been interested in getting to know more intimately. Meagan didn't have anything against dating divorcées, but she'd made it a rule to steer clear of men with kids. She liked children, for the most part, but with her crazy schedule and rather poor track record with relationships, kids were a complication she hadn't wanted to deal with. She'd always thought she'd have one of her own someday, she mused, resisting an impulse to press a hand to her slightly throbbing surgical scar, but she'd never wanted to risk hurting anyone else's children by being only a temporary part of their life.

Fortunately, that wasn't an issue here, she assured herself, accepting a dessert plate from Alice with a smile and a murmured thanks. She and Alice were the friends, with Seth merely a bystander. She'd done her best to warn Alice that she'd have little free time once she returned to work, but maybe Alice could still drop by on the occasional weekend afternoon for a swim. Meagan would probably hardly see Seth at all.

Not that she minded seeing him, she thought, casting a glance at him over her coffee cup. He was certainly pleasant to look at.

She didn't linger after dessert. Following her father's instructions, Alice began to clear away the dishes. She and Meagan said their good nights at the table, agreeing to meet at ten the next morning for the shopping outing. Leaving Alice to her chores, Seth walked Meagan to the door.

"You're sure you're up to the shopping trip?"

She gave a firm nod. "Very sure. Actually, I'm looking forward to it. I'd find an excuse to get out tomorrow even if I hadn't volunteered to take Alice."

His deep, rich chuckle made her swallow rather hard, for some reason. "Getting a little stir crazy?"

"Getting a *lot* stir crazy," she admitted with a wrinkle of her nose. "If I hadn't had Alice's visits to look forward to, I'd probably have been climbing the walls by now."

"She said you work at River City Medical Center?"

She nodded. "Yes, I—"

"Dad! Waldo's knocked over a whole pile of stuff in the garage. You'd better come help me."

Alice's distant shout sounded more exasperated than frantic. Seth sighed heavily. "I guess I'd better go help her with the disaster dog. I've still got to find out how he escaped the backyard. It was very nice meeting you, Meagan."

"Nice meeting you, too. Thank you for dinner."

"I hope you can join us again sometime."

He was probably just being polite. She smiled and replied vaguely, "That would be lovely. Good night, Seth."

"Good night, Mea—"

"Dad!"

"I'm coming, Alice." Giving Meagan a rueful smile, he closed the front door behind her when she stepped outside.

The short walk to her house was much easier without a squirming mutt in her arms. The air was cooling and deepening dusk cast purple shadows on the street around her. She had enjoyed the spontaneous dinner party, she thought as she pulled her keys from her jeans pocket to unlock her front door. She really had been suffering from cabin fever lately. The only time she'd left home this past week was for a couple hours that morning to see her doctor and then visit briefly with her mom and grandmother. She could hardly even remember the last time she'd spent an evening with an attractive, amusing man.

But no, that didn't sound right. She'd shared a meal with Alice and her dad, hardly with Seth alone.

Maybe it had been too long since she'd been out for an adult evening, considering the little tingle still lingering inside her as a result of Seth's parting smile.

"Honey, we have to do something with that hair!"

Alice lifted a hand self-consciously to her riotous mass of curls in response to Madison's blunt assessment. "I guess it needs a trim."

Madison laughed softly and patted Alice's shoulder. "Sweetie, you need more than a trim. You need a good cut and style. The walk-in place upstairs is hit-and-miss, but I know which stylists there can be trusted. Let's get up and see how long the waiting list is."

Frowning, Meagan followed in her younger sister's wake, as she usually did when Madison took charge. "Um, Maddie? I'm not sure we should get her hair cut without her father's permission."

Alice looked over her shoulder with a frown. "I'm not a baby, Meagan. Dad lets me choose how to wear my own hair—well, as long as I don't get a mohawk or dye it purple or anything," she added with a little laugh.

Because Meagan had no intention of sanctioning either of those options, she decided maybe a simple haircut wouldn't be so bad.

As she had expected, Madison and Alice hit it off immediately. No surprise. Everyone liked Madison, with her ebullient warmth and contagious laugh. A second year psychiatry resident, Madison wanted to specialize in adolescents. Their brother said it was because Madison had never really grown up, herself, an accusation with which Madison cheerfully agreed.

Slim and animated, Madison had shoulder length hair that was naturally the same rather mousy brown as Meagan's. Like Meagan, she dyed it a more interesting shade, though Madison had gone even blonder than Meagan's honey color. Madison's eyes were a shade lighter blue and her features, at least in Meagan's opinion, were a little more classically pretty. Madison never seemed to run out of energy or enthusiasm, which had come in handy during medical school and her first year of residency.

They were lucky enough to arrive at the walk-in salon at a lull in business. One of the stylists Madison knew and trusted just happened to be available. Madison and the stylist, Kiera, put their heads together for a lengthy and serious-looking consultation while glancing sideways at Alice, who shifted her feet self-consciously.

"You know you don't have to let them do anything you don't want," Meagan reminded the girl.

Alice nodded resolutely. "Madison's so pretty. She'll know what I should do."

And then she added quickly, "I'd trust you, too, of course. You're pretty, too."

Meagan laughed, patting Alice's arm to show there'd been no offense taken. Meagan, too, thought her younger sister was beautiful. "Thank you, but Madison's the one who knows all the latest styles and fashions. That's why I asked her to join us today."

They both looked at Madison, who had dressed in a

trendy top and skinny jeans with wedge-heeled sandals for their shopping excursion. Typically, Meagan's look was more classic—a crisp white shirt with jeans and comfortable loafers. The traditional style worked for her, but Alice needed a guide for younger fashion.

Leaving Alice in Kiera's capable hands, Meagan and Madison sat side by side in the waiting area.

"So, how good-looking is Alice's dad?" Madison asked with a grin.

Meagan lifted an eyebrow. "Why?"

Madison laughed. "He must be cute for you to agree to spend a morning shopping with his teenage daughter. You've never really liked shopping."

"I was glad to have an excuse to get out of the house for a few hours, but mostly I just wanted to help Alice. She's a very sweet girl. This has nothing to do with Seth."

"Oh. He's *very* cute."

Meagan studied her sister in exasperation. "What brought you to that conclusion?"

Her expression mischievous, Madison replied, "I could tell by the way you said his name. Seth. My guess is that he's quite the catch."

Meagan sighed. "If you're interested, I'll arrange an introduction."

"I've got no time for a fella right now, but there's nothing holding *you* back. Go for it, sis."

Meagan couldn't help smiling in return. It was hard not to be amused when Madison teased so good-naturedly. "He's just a neighbor. A busy single father, at that. You know how I feel about dating guys with children. Too many potential complications in my schedule that's already hectic enough."

"Chicken."

"Cluck, cluck."

"You're hopeless, Meagan. What's it going to take to make you pay a little attention to your own needs, for a change?" Madison's smile disappeared abruptly. "You nearly let yourself die because you wouldn't stop long enough to take care of your own health."

Because she knew her illness had frightened her sister, Meagan replied patiently. "I didn't almost die, Maddie. I went to Meilin as soon as I realized I needed attention."

"It took you too long to reach that realization. Because you were so busy taking care of everyone else."

"Look who's talking, Dr. Baker. Who's training to spend the rest of her life taking care of troubled kids?"

"A job," Madison said with a wave of her hand. "I don't plan to spend my every waking moment doing it. That was one reason I chose psychiatry over surgery, remember? Better hours."

Knowing career demands had much less to do with her sister's choice than the calling of her heart, Meagan didn't even bother to argue that point. "This is an academic conversation, anyway. Seth and I spent all of an hour together, and that hour was mostly focused on Alice. It's not as though he asked me out or anything."

"And if he should?"

Meagan shrugged, trying to hide the little ripple of nerves that coursed through her at the suggestion. "I doubt he will. I'm Alice's friend, not Seth's."

"Mmm."

She didn't even ask what her sister meant by that enigmatic murmur. Instead, she glanced toward the chair where Alice was being worked on. "Ouch. That looks like a lot of hair falling."

Madison shrugged dismissively. "She needed a good cut. She has pretty hair, but you couldn't even see her face in that mop of curls. Wonder how her dad feels about contact lenses."

"We're not getting her contact lenses today."

Laughing, Madison shook her head. "I'm not sure we could arrange that on such short notice, anyway. Just saying."

Meagan was relieved that the conversation had drifted away from her dating life—or lack of one. Maybe she privately agreed that it was time for her to get back into the social scene, and had thought about doing so quite a bit during the past few days but that didn't mean she regarded every single man she met as a viable partner. No matter how intriguing Alice's father might be.

Seth arrived home just over half an hour before he was scheduled to drive Alice to her party. He was rather proud of himself for concluding his work early enough that he didn't have to make a mad rush to get her there. He had time to change and have a cold glass of tea before they walked out the door.

"Alice?" he called out as he walked into the kitchen from the garage, dropping his car keys on the counter and setting his brief case on the kitchen table. "I'm home."

"Hi, Dad," she called from another room. "Just a sec, I'm almost ready."

He could hear Waldo barking from out in the backyard. The dog must have heard Seth's car. Seth decided to spend a little time with the mutt while Alice was at her party. It wouldn't hurt to get a head start on those obedience lessons, he figured, and he knew the dog would enjoy the extra attention, though Alice had probably played with him all afternoon after her shopping excursion. She sure loved that dopey—

His thoughts drifted off to stunned silence when his daughter walked through the kitchen door.

She made a slow rotation in front of him, her smile self-conscious and satisfied. "How do I look?"

"You look...like a teenager." His voice sounded a bit husky even to him.

Her smile flashed even brighter, braces gleaming. "Sweet."

He couldn't decide at first exactly what was different about her. There seemed to be several changes. Her hair, for example. The wild mop she had always bemoaned but he'd thought impishly cute had been shortened, layered and tamed into softer curls framing her face and just brushing her nape. While still youthful, the new style was a little more sophisticated than before.

She was wearing makeup. Not enough for him to object to—just a touch of glitter on her eyelids and a little clear gloss on her pretty pink mouth.

Her new dress was a halter style, baring her slender shoulders and arms, but still modestly styled. A yellow satin cummerbund with a jaunty bow separated the black surplice top from the flared white skirt with three rows of narrow black ribbon at the hem. Her shoes were black, with lots of straps and low platform bottoms that gave the illusion of heels even though they weren't too high for her age. All in all, a very pretty and appropriate outfit—for a teenager, he thought again, swallowing hard.

Her smile wavered a little. "Don't you like it, Dad?"

"You look beautiful," he told her simply.

She beamed again. "Really?"

"Yes. Uh—you couldn't find a ruffled pink dress with puffy sleeves and a lace pinafore?"

"Daddy."

He laughed wryly. "Just teasing, sweetheart. It's not easy

for a dad to admit his little girl is growing up. I guess we'll have to see about an appointment for those contact lenses you've been begging for. We'll get you some as soon as school's out for the summer, which will give you plenty of time to get used to them before fall semester starts."

She almost bounced in pleasure, pushing her glasses up on her nose as if in eagerness to be rid of them. "I was going to remind you about that. Madison said I have pretty brown eyes and it's a shame to hide them behind glasses."

"Madison is right." He opened the fridge and pulled out a canned drink. "So you had a good time on your girls' outing?"

He'd already talked with her since she'd returned; he'd made her promise she would call as soon as she was home safely. She'd chattered excitedly about the shopping excursion until he'd had to disconnect the call and return to his client.

"I had a great time. Madison is really fun and cool and she knows everything about fashion. And Meagan always makes me laugh with her little comments about stuff. I got my hair cut and then I tried on a lot of dresses and then we had Chinese for lunch—Meagan treated us—and then Madison bought me this bracelet from a little booth out in the center of the mall."

She showed off a band of small black stones tied with a yellow ribbon to match her dress. "I paid for the dress and shoes and haircut with my debit card, like you told me. And I stayed on the budget you gave me. The dress was on sale! Twenty percent off. Madison says she never pays full price when she can find a sale."

"Well, that's—"

"And Meagan said she'll take me shopping again sometime if I want her to. I said a lot of my clothes are getting too little because I'm getting taller and I'm going to need some new shirts and shorts and stuff for summer."

"Nina can take you shopping whenever you need to go," he reminded her, hoping she wasn't expecting Meagan and Madison to be her personal shoppers now. "I'll talk to her about giving you more leeway in choosing your own clothes. Or I can take you, though I've got to admit I don't know a lot about what's in style for girls your age."

She waved a hand, looking unenthused by either prospect. "Anyway, at lunch we were talking and I said some of my friends think you're hot, which is, you know, kind of gross, and Madison laughed and said she'd already heard you were cute. And then she looked at Meagan and laughed some more, so I think Meagan told her you're cute. Which you are, for a dad, I guess."

Seth had gotten totally lost in that rush of words, but he pulled one phrase out of the babble. *Meagan told her you're cute.*

Seriously? He sipped his cold soda thoughtfully, a nice feeling expanding inside his chest. Meagan thought he was…?

Scowling, he set the can on the counter with a thump that made drops of cola spray from the opening. He wiped up the spill with a sponge, berating himself for acting like a teenager, himself.

"I'll run up and change into jeans, then I'll drive you to the party," he said, concentrating on the business at hand. "Don't forget to take your cell phone in case you need to reach me for any reason before I'm supposed to pick you up."

She rolled her eyes a little—the long-suffering teen expression more marked now that he could see her face better. "I'll be fine, Daddy. We'll have plenty of chaperones."

He trusted in that. He sent his daughter to a highly-respected private school with strict rules of behavior and an outstanding academic record. The administrators approved parties and social activities for the students, but they were well supervised. Uniforms were required for classes. The dress code for parties was more lenient, but attendees were still expected to dress tastefully whether for one of the casual jeans-and-tees events or a dressier affair like tonight's.

He was doing his best to make sure his daughter made it safely through these risky years, he thought wryly on his way to his bedroom. Which didn't guarantee, of course, that she wouldn't go wild or get into the wrong crowd or all those other possibilities that would keep him awake nights if he dwelled on them.

He was relieved that Meagan and her sister had helped Alice choose an appropriate outfit. Not that he'd worried too much that they wouldn't. Judging from Nina's initial assessment and his own impressions of Meagan so far, she was rather conservative, herself, and could be trusted to serve as a good role model for Alice. At least, he hoped he was right about that.

And she thought he was—

He sighed heavily.

Apparently, it had been much too long since he'd been with a woman.

Meagan felt a bit self-conscious entering the school auditorium Tuesday evening. She figured most parents and students at the private academy knew each other, and would probably wonder about this stranger who had wandered in to attend the junior high choir concert. The turnout was certainly good. She had arrived almost twenty minutes before the program was to begin and the parking lot was already almost full.

Accepting a program printed on a folded sheet of red paper, she entered the auditorium. Rows of fold-down wooden seats arranged on a sloping concrete floor faced an elevated stage draped in black and burgundy velvet. Most of the seats were filled. The noise level was quite high, with people talking and laughing, children chattering, a few toddlers shrieking, almost drowning out the generic recorded music playing from surrounding speakers. She was glad she'd decided not to dress too formally; her green knit top and casual khaki pants fit in very nicely with the other attendees.

She had deliberated for quite a while before she'd decided to attend this event. Alice had mentioned at lunch Saturday that she would be singing in a choir concert this evening. She'd said she would have to wear her required choir dress but she would wear her new shoes with it. Rather wistfully, she had added that her father wouldn't be able to attend this end-of-the-year concert.

"He's only missed a couple of my school programs before," she said quickly, in case Meagan or Madison formed a poor opinion of her beloved father. "He hates having to miss them, but he said he'll be in a big meeting in Hot Springs Tuesday and he doesn't think he'll be back in time for the concert. They always start at six because the teachers want to get home early. Sometimes my grandparents from Heber Springs come to my concerts and things, but they can't come this time. But Nina's going to be there. She said she loves to hear me sing."

Meagan had told herself there was no need for her to attend the concert. Alice would probably be perfectly happy with Nina there to appreciate her performance; she seemed very fond of the housekeeper who'd been employed by Seth for several years. Would it really mean much to the girl to have her neighbor—a woman she'd known for only a week—applauding in the audience?

But somehow Meagan had found herself in her car that evening, headed for the school. As hard as Alice had tried to hide it, she was obviously disappointed that her dad wouldn't be there. Meagan doubted that she made a suitable replacement, but maybe Alice would appreciate having another friend in the audience, anyway. Besides, it was another excuse to get out of the house for an evening. And how bored was she getting that a junior high choir concert sounded more interesting than another night of reading and TV?

She really needed to get back to work soon.

Thinking she might sit with the housekeeper during the concert, Meagan had looked for Nina when she'd arrived, but couldn't find her in the crowd. She assumed Nina had taken a seat close to the front.

Because she hadn't wanted to wander up and down the aisles searching for Nina, she chose a seat closer to the door instead. She thought she'd be able to see well from there, though a child a few rows ahead of her kept standing up in his seat. Other than the empty seat next to her, the section was full. People around her laughed and talked and waved at acquaintances across the auditorium. Feeling a bit like an imposter among all the friends and family members waiting for the concert to begin, Meagan smiled and nodded to the older woman sitting beside her, who murmured a greeting in return then turned away to chat with her companions.

"Excuse me, ma'am, is this seat taken?"

In response to the polite question only minutes before the concert was to begin, she glanced up automatically from the program she'd been studying to assure the speaker that the seat was free. The words died when she saw who stood in the aisle, smiling down at her.

Seth's hair was a little tousled, she noticed, and he looked just a bit disheveled, as if he'd rushed to get there. He wore a beautifully tailored gray suit, more formal than most of the more casually garbed audience, but he'd loosened the blue-and-silver tie at the collar.

Definitely cute, she thought, remembering the teasing conversation with her sister. And when he took her up on her gestured invitation and dropped into the seat beside her, he was close enough that their arms brushed when he shifted his weight.

The concert had just gotten even more interesting.

Chapter Three

"I didn't expect to see you here," Meagan and Seth said at almost exactly the same time.

They laughed, then she said, "Alice said you had to work late tonight."

"I was able to get away a little earlier than I expected. I might have driven a little too fast to make it here on time. I saw you when I walked in just now and I had to look twice to make sure it really was you."

"Alice told me about the concert during our outing Saturday. She invited me to come and it sounded like fun."

"You *must* be getting cabin fever if this sounded like fun."

The unwitting repetition of her own earlier thoughts made her laugh again. "You could be right."

He wasn't smiling now. "Or maybe you were being nice. You didn't think I'd be here, so you wanted to make sure Alice had more than our housekeeper supporting her in the audience."

She didn't want him to think Alice had said anything at all critical of him, or had deliberately played on Meagan's sympathies. "Alice made it very clear you wanted to be here, Seth. She said you almost never miss any of her programs or performances. I didn't come because I felt sorry for her or anything like that."

His lips quirked a little, as though he were almost amused by her reassurances. "I appreciate that. I can't help feeling guilty when work threatens to interfere with Alice's plans."

"I'm sure every working parent, married or single, struggles with that guilt." Which was why she wasn't entirely sure she should ever take on that responsibility, she mused as the overhead lights blinked to notify the noisy audience that the program was about to begin. Had she been back at work, it would have been very difficult for her to attend a six o'clock school program—not without reshuffling her usual work schedule, anyway.

The velvet curtains parted on stage and an expectant hush fell over the audience—except for one toddler who wanted to "go pee pee right *now!*" A few giggles broke out in response to the vocal demand, but most eyes were focused on the stage when the performers filed out from the wings to encouraging applause. The boys wore white shirts, black pants and black vests, and the girls were in long black dresses with three-quarter sleeves and white satin waist sashes. They all looked very much alike, Meagan thought with a frown, but then she smiled when she saw Alice on the second row.

Squirming a little in the not-particularly-comfortable auditorium seat, Seth propped his elbow on the wooden armrest between them just as Meagan leaned a bit that way. Their shoulders bumped, hands brushing on the armrest. Both straightened quickly, murmuring apologies and looking intently toward the stage. Meagan moistened her lips, a little shaken by that momentary contact. It had been a long time since a man's fleeting touch had made her pulse rate trip. She had to admit it was a nice feeling—even though she wasn't at all sure she should be reacting that way to this particular man. Didn't she have enough complications in her busy life?

She focused intently on the reason she was there, rather than the imagined warmth emanating from the man sitting so close to her. It was an interesting concert. The choir performed a mix of classical pieces, oldies and more recent pop numbers—whatever the director had been able to afford to license for performance, Meagan figured in amusement. The kids were pretty good overall, though occasionally a note escaped that should not have been made by human vocal cords. The doting parents and grandparents in attendance didn't seem to mind; they clapped as enthusiastically for the bad notes as the good.

"Alice has a very pretty voice," she commented to Seth after one of the numbers. Alice had sung a couple of solo lines, and though nerves shook her voice a little, she still had a very nice tone.

"She got that from her mother," Seth admitted ruefully. "I can't sing a lick."

Meagan spent the time during the next number wondering how Seth felt about his ex-wife. She'd heard little animosity in his voice on the few occasions he'd spoken of her. Had the split been amicable or was he hiding bitterness for his daughter's sake? Had his heart been broken or hardened or relatively unscathed? Did he still love his wife? Had he ever, really?

Realizing she was indulging in idle speculation—a game of solitaire gossip—she told herself those questions were absolutely none of her business. She concentrated intently on the remainder of the concert, making a rather futile effort to keep her attention from wandering…elsewhere.

"To Alice. The star of the Pulaski Preparatory Academy junior high choir." Seth lifted his plastic tumbler of fountain soda as he made the teasing toast a half hour after the concert's end.

Brushed by the curls of her saucy new haircut, Alice's cheeks reddened with embarrassed pleasure. She pushed her glasses up on her nose and muttered, "I'm not the star, Daddy. I only had two solo lines. Andrea Merchant is like the star of the choir. She always gets the long solos."

"I like your voice better than hers," Meagan asserted loyally as she dipped a french fry in ketchup. "She leans too heavily on melisma for my taste. I know it's the style these days, but I think it's overused."

"Melisma?" Seth wasn't sure he'd heard that term before.

"Stretching a single syllable with several notes," Alice supplied quickly, her reciting tone suggesting it was a definition she'd learned in class. "You know, like ba-a-a-a-a-by."

She warbled the word in illustration, hitting several notes in the process.

Seth nodded to indicate he understood. "That technique is overused these days. I didn't know what it was called, but I often wish the singer would just pick a note and stick with it."

Meagan and Alice launched into a discussion of current music stars and their singing styles, and Meagan proved to be quite up-to-date on contemporary music, though she admitted she didn't follow the younger musical acts as much. Alice, whose taste in music had always been eclectic, made a snide comment about the teen-idol performers most popular with her classmates. Watching her, Seth tried to hide his amusement at her obvious attempt to appear more mature than the other young teens in front of Meagan.

His smile faded when he noted that Alice seemed to be imitating some of Meagan's mannerisms, following the older woman's example in cutting her cheeseburger into neat quarters before eating it, dabbing her napkin tidily at the corners of her mouth after each bite. He really didn't mind that Alice had befriended the nice neighbor, but he hoped she wasn't getting too attached. For all he knew, Meagan could lose interest in the kid once her sick leave ended and she returned to her former schedule. Not many single women Meagan's age wanted to spend time with a thirteen-year-old—not even one as clever and sweet as his daughter, he thought, well aware of his bias.

It had been his idea to invite Meagan to join them for dinner after the concert. He'd figured she hadn't eaten that early, and she'd confirmed his guess. He'd told her he'd promised Alice cheeseburgers and fries at her favorite burger joint after the concert—a rare treat, since he tried to promote healthy eating most evenings. At the time he'd offered, he hadn't been sure he'd even be at the concert, but he'd promised to take her to dinner as soon as he could get there afterward. He was relieved he'd been able to make it to the event, though it had required almost superhuman effort to make it there on time.

Meagan had hesitated when he'd extended the invitation to her, but once again Alice had persuaded her to accept. He figured the least he could do was buy Meagan a burger since she had been nice enough to attend Alice's concert. As kind as her intention had been, it still grated that it had been partially motivated by pity because poor Alice had a busy, working dad. Even though Meagan had assured him she understood the demands of single parenthood, she'd still felt obliged to fill in for him tonight, apparently. He was doubly glad he'd been able to get there, both for Alice's sake and to prove to Meagan that he really did put his daughter above all his other responsibilities. He couldn't say why it was so important for her, in particular, to see that.

He'd invited Nina to dinner, too, but Nina declined, saying her favorite television program was on that evening and she didn't want to miss it. Seth hadn't missed Nina's little nod of approval when he'd included Meagan in the outing. Nina had dropped a couple of little hints about what a nice woman Meagan seemed to be and how well she and Alice got along and wasn't it interesting that such a pretty single woman—emphasis on single—lived so close to his new house?

Seth was more amused than annoyed by his longtime housekeeper's blatant matchmaking. Meagan seemed to be exactly the type of woman he should date, actually. Attractive, intelligent, and she liked his daughter. He had to admit he had quite a physical reaction to her warm smiles, and he enjoyed watching the emotions dancing through her expressive blue eyes. He'd been keenly aware of her sitting so close to him in the darkened auditorium, her arm bumping his when they applauded, her eyes meeting his in the shadows when they found something mutually amusing.

He'd been aware of the curious glances they'd gotten from his acquaintances among the other parents. They had probably assumed he and Meagan had arranged to meet there. Had that been true, it would have been the first time he'd attended one of his daughter's school activities with anyone other than his housekeeper or, occasionally, Alice's maternal grandparents.

He wouldn't mind getting to know Meagan better—on a one-to-one basis—but what if it didn't work out? Would

Alice be disappointed yet again? Or, equally worrisome, what if it *did* work out? Was Alice really prepared to share her father's attention, when he had to ration his time with her as it was? And speaking of time, did he really have enough of it to divide between his daughter and a more adult relationship?

"I felt so sorry for Jeffrey when his voice cracked in the middle of his solo line," Alice said, calling Seth's attention abruptly back to the conversation. "Jeffrey was so embarrassed. He's really nice, in a shy sort of way."

Something about her self-conscious tone caught Seth's notice. Did his daughter have a crush on a boy in her choir? Was she old enough to have crushes already? Did he have to start worrying about that now? She wasn't anywhere near old enough to have a boyfriend, and if she thought she was going to date at thirteen she had another think coming!

And hadn't he just been sitting there worrying about the consequences of a relationship with a woman he hardly knew? One who might not even be interested in going out with him anyway?

They were quite a pair, he and his daughter. For now, it was probably best for them both to stay single.

"I had a good time tonight, Dad. Thanks for the burger. And for letting me have the hot fudge sundae for dessert. It was so good!"

Tossing his keys on the counter as they walked into the house a while later, Seth ruffled his daughter's hair affectionately. "You're welcome, Roo. You deserved it after that great concert."

She wrapped her arms around his waist for a big hug. "I'm glad you could be there."

"So am I, kiddo. Though there will still be times when

my work will interfere with other things," he warned her candidly. "I have to make a living for us."

"I know, Dad," she said, rolling her eyes a little as she stepped back. "I'm not a little kid, I understand about work commitments. But I'm glad you could come tonight, anyway."

"Me, too." He picked up a stack of mail Nina had left on the counter for him and flipped through the envelopes. Bills, mostly. Credit card and insurance offers. A postcard from his favorite men's clothing store announcing an annual sale on suits. He'd have to check that out, he could use a new suit for summer.

Slitting open a small, square, cream-colored envelope, he drew out a folded card and scanned it quickly. He groaned.

Alice looked around from the sink, where she was cleaning Waldo's water dish and filling it with fresh water for the night while the dog whined impatiently from the other side of the back door. "What is it, Dad?"

"It's a reminder for a fancy charity thing I'm supposed to attend. It's a week from Friday. Clever of DeAnna to send out reminders ten days ahead, this thing's been scheduled for months and I'd forgotten all about it."

"You hate fancy charity things," Alice said sympathetically.

She knew him well. He nodded grimly. "I do. But I've got to go to this one. DeAnna is the managing partner's new wife. He's going to be checking who supports her at this."

"Then I guess you have to go."

"Yeah," he grumbled. "I guess I do."

She glanced at the Norman Rockwell calendar attached to the side of the refrigerator with a heavy-duty magnet, the calendar Nina used to keep track of the family's schedule. "It's already written down. You just haven't looked."

"Yeah, I'm sure it's on my personal calendar, too. Just been too busy lately to look that far ahead. I'd have seen it eventually."

"That's the night of my sleepover party at Gayla's house for her thirteenth birthday. Her mom's hiring a party planner and we're going to learn how to decorate cupcakes all fancy like they do on the food channel shows. We're going to do piping and everything."

"Sounds like fun. Don't eat too many sweets," he said automatically, still scanning the party reminder.

A gusty sigh was her response as she carried the bowl of water to the door. He reached out to open the storm door for her, using his body to block Waldo's eager attempt to dash inside to cause chaos. Seth was still skeptical that obedience classes would work any miracles with this particular dog. But the instructor had assured him when he'd signed up Waldo for the classes that Labradors were usually quick to learn. Waldo appeared to be mostly yellow Lab, though Seth suspected a slightly more rambunctious breed might be mixed into the bloodlines.

"So, Dad, have you asked anyone to go with you to the fancy thing yet?" Alice inquired when she came back inside a short while later. "You know, a date?"

"Well, no. I told you, I forgot all about it."

"You can't go without a date," she scolded, shaking her head. "That would make you look all pathetic, like you don't have a social life."

He resisted pointing out the obvious fact that he did not have a social life. He was too overtaxed by his work life and his home life.

"Maybe I'll ask Susan if she wants to go with me," he

mused, naming a woman he'd dated a few times on a very casual basis.

Alice made a gagging noise, pantomiming a finger down her throat.

He frowned. She had met Susan only once, and that was for maybe fifteen minutes. Susan had ridden with them while he'd driven Alice to a friend's house before he and Susan attended a holiday party early in December. Susan had been perfectly nice to Alice, and Alice had responded politely—as she was expected to do with adults. It occurred to Seth only now that Alice had never mentioned Susan since.

"What's wrong with her?" he asked, genuinely curious.

"She's so fake. Fake tan, fake hair, fake eye color, fake boobs."

A little shocked that his young daughter had noticed those things—kids grew up way too fast these days!—he scolded, "That's not very nice, Alice."

"Sorry. But it's true."

Well, yeah, he thought with a little wince. It sort of was. Susan was unabashedly vain about her appearance, and didn't mind resorting to artifice to enhance it but it paid off for her. She looked great. And she was quite pleasant company, though he admitted uncomfortably that she rarely crossed his mind when he wasn't in need of a convenient escort for some professional function. He doubted that she thought of him any more often. They were casual friends, nothing more, and that suited both of them.

"She's not so bad. She said she thought you were very sweet."

Of course, she'd said it in a slightly patronizing tone that Alice would have hated. Susan made no pretense to be the maternal type.

Looking a little abashed, Alice shrugged. "I guess she wasn't so bad, really, but so not your type, Dad."

"I'm not sure I have a type right now."

"What about Meagan?"

He paused in the process of getting a glass for a drink of water. "Uh—what *about* Meagan?"

His daughter gave him a wide-eyed, innocent smile. "You could always ask her to the charity thing. I bet she'd go. She's pretty bored, being on sick leave and all."

Hardly a flattering reason for Meagan to accept an invitation with him, he thought, then quickly shook his head. "I don't know, Alice. I hardly know her."

"You've had two dinners with her," she reminded him unnecessarily. "You seemed to like her fine. You smiled a lot with her."

"I do like her. Your friend is quite nice." He stressed the "your." "But that doesn't mean she would be interested in going with me to a charity ball."

"You could ask her and see. Or I could ask her for you. I'm going swimming at her house after school Thursday."

"I'll do my own asking," he said hastily. "Don't you even think about it."

She poked out her lip a little, as if she couldn't see a problem with her making his social arrangements, but she nodded. "Okay. So you'll ask her? I'll give you her cell phone number. She gave it to me."

"I'll consider it." Maybe he would ask Meagan. Maybe she wouldn't mind being invited at a fairly late date to attend a rather exclusive social event with him. He'd make it clear when he asked—if he asked—that there would be no hard feelings if she declined, that she and Alice could still be friends, if she wanted, and that they could still be cordial neighbors. No pressure.

Still—

"If you're trying to be a matchmaker for me and Meagan, you can forget it," he warned his daughter. "I'm not looking for a girlfriend right now, okay? You know how busy I am. There's just no time for a relationship. I want to spend as much of my free time as I can with you."

"I'm not matchmaking," she protested too quickly and a bit too loudly. "I just thought you'd have fun with Meagan at the charity thing. Geez."

"Okay, fine. Just remember what I said."

"But it's not like you couldn't get married again or something, if you wanted to, Dad. You don't have to stay single just because of me. I mean, I know you and Mom are never going to get back together."

"You're right, honey. That's not going to happen."

"It's okay," she assured him. "I know all about some people not being able to live together. You and Mom are too different. I love you both, but you'd never be happy living the way she does and she wouldn't be happy living here with us. I want you both to be happy."

Sometimes his daughter's quaint mix of innocence and maturity broke his heart. This was one of those times. "Thank you, Alice. That's all we want for you, too."

"I know, Daddy. So you'll ask Meagan to the thing?"

The segue made him a little uncomfortable, but he nodded. "I'll ask her. That doesn't mean she'll accept. Which is perfectly okay. Promise me you won't say a word to her about it either way."

She frowned a little but nodded reluctantly. "I promise."

"Okay. Now, you'd better get busy with whatever you have to do before bedtime. It's still a school night."

"I don't have any homework tonight. But I'll go change into my pj's and lay out my clothes for tomorrow."

Asking Meagan to the charity thing could be a bad idea on so many levels, Seth thought as his daughter headed for her room. Yet picturing himself attending with Meagan made him dread the event a little less. Assuming she agreed to go with him, of course.

Meagan hung up her phone Wednesday afternoon feeling slightly bemused. Her mother and sister looked up from their coffee with interest when she rejoined them at her mother's kitchen table, having taken her call in another room for privacy. With Meagan still on sick leave for another week and Madison free for a rare weekday afternoon, they had taken advantage of the chance to get together for coffee and cake.

"Well?" Madison prompted before Meagan was even settled comfortably in her chair again. "That was obviously a call from a guy. We want details, don't we, Mom?"

Their mother shook her head with a laugh. "Don't get me in the middle of this. I'm not asking any questions."

"Well, I am. Who was it, Meagan?"

Meagan sighed gustily. "Not that it's any of your business, but it was Seth Llewellyn."

"Alice's dad?"

"Yes."

"And?"

"And…he asked me to attend a charity dance with him next Friday night. Nothing serious, he just needed a date."

"Ah hah!"

"Ah hah, *what?*"

"I thought you were interested in him," Madison said smugly. "You said he's cute and you've been spending time with his kid. Meagan's got a crush."

"Don't be so juvenile, Maddie."

"Just being observant," her sister retorted. "Your cheeks were all pink and your eyes were all shiny when you came back from your call. You're so interested."

Meagan felt her cheeks warm again. So maybe she'd been a little flustered by Seth's call. She wasn't going to deny that there'd been a few sparks between them, which she had suspected weren't all on her side. But she hadn't expected him to call today.

He had apologized for asking with only a little more than a week's notice, and had made a somewhat rehearsed-sounding speech about how he would understand perfectly if she turned him down. It had been that rather charmingly self-conscious assurance that had prompted her to accept despite any reservations she might have about going out with her single-dad neighbor.

"Like I said, he needed a date for a professional function," she muttered, picking up her cup of cooling coffee. "I got the impression he had forgotten about the event."

"And your name just happened to pop into his mind."

"Or maybe I was the only person he thought might be available on rather short notice," she shot back at her sister. "Really, Madison, aren't we beyond teasing each other when we have a date? We're hardly naive teenagers still all giggly about spending time with boys."

That said, Meagan turned firmly to their mom. "Is Meemaw eating any better since her doctor changed her meds?"

Their grandmother had visited with them for a few minutes when Meagan and Madison arrived half an hour earlier but she'd excused herself then for a nap, asking her daughter to assist her to bed. She was spending more and more time in her bed these days, despite her daughter's efforts to keep her active and engaged.

"Maybe she's eating a little better. Not a lot."

Teasing forgotten, Meagan and Madison shared a glance in response to their mother's worried expression. Their mom was reluctant to admit that her own mother was failing rather quickly from congestive heart failure and other ailments.

The woman Meagan and Madison had always known as "Meemaw" was in her eighties, having been somewhat older than average when her only child was born. A lifetime of self-neglect had taken its toll on her health; their grandmother had always been the type to take care of everyone but herself, Meagan thought with a little wince. Apparently, it was a genetic trait. Meagan would have to do better about making sure she took time for her own health needs from now on.

As should her mom, she thought, looking in concern at her overextended parent. Mom was too thin, she thought, studying the slender frame outlined by her mother's casual outfit of jeans and a Doctor Who T-shirt Mitch had given her as a joke. Their mom loved that silly T-shirt and wore it all the time around the house. But was it a bit looser on her today than it had been a few weeks earlier?

"You have to take care of yourself, too, Mom. Between your part-time job and serving as full-time caregiver for Meemaw, you're wearing yourself out. Not to mention the way you've been fretting about me since my surgery, despite my assurances that I'm healing rapidly. I wish you'd let us hire someone to help you."

All three siblings had offered to pitch in to hire round-the-clock help for their mother and grandmother. Their late father had left his widow in decent financial shape, but she still worked ten hours a week keeping books for a little insurance office owned by a longtime friend. Having worked as a CPA her entire adult life, she missed having a job outside the home, she'd admitted. Meemaw's health care plan paid for someone to come in a few hours a week—long enough for her daughter to escape to her job for those few hours—but anything more than that would have to come out-of-pocket, an expense frugal LaDonna wasn't sure she could justify.

As she always did, their mother shook her head firmly. "All of you are still paying off medical school loans. You need your money for your own futures. Meemaw and I are getting along fine for now."

"I paid off my loans last year," Meagan reminded her. She made a healthy salary as a surgeon in the teaching hospital, as her mother was well aware. She could probably make even more in private practice, but she enjoyed teaching and she earned enough for her needs and then some.

"Yes, but now you have a house payment."

"Which I can afford. It isn't as if I bought a mansion."

"I know, dear, but you should put some money away for your retirement. It gets here before you know it. And you should take some time to travel and have a little fun while you're still young. You've worked so hard. You deserve a few luxuries. You all do. I'm so proud of my kids."

As if on cue, there was a thump on the kitchen door. Without waiting for a response, Mitchell entered in his usual rush, tossing his keys on the kitchen counter with a noisy clatter and leaning over to kiss his mother with a resounding smack. "Hi, Mom. Coffee still hot? You saved me some cake, right?"

Delighted, she rose immediately from her chair. "Of course I did. I'm so glad you could make the time to stop by." She had called him to tell him his sisters were there and to see if he could join them for a brief visit. "It's so nice to have all my kids home at one time for a change."

Grinning at his sisters, Mitch dropped into an empty chair at the table. "When you said there was cake, I knew

I'd better get here fast or these vultures would gobble it all up. I just happened to have a couple free hours this afternoon, though I have to get back to the hospital by five."

"Then we'll enjoy you while we have you," his adoring mother replied, setting a cup of coffee and a huge slice of german chocolate cake in front of him.

"What's up with you two?" Mitch asked his sisters, pushing his perpetually-shaggy dark blond hair out of his face as he picked up his fork.

"Meagan's got a new boyfriend," Madison replied immediately with a mischievous smirk. "He's a single dad, so she could end up a stepmom."

"Madison!"

Mitch eyed Meagan's annoyed expression. "A single dad? Thought that was against your rules, sis."

"Rules go out the window when 'twue wuv' comes in," Madison teased.

Exhaling heavily, Meagan rose to refill her coffee cup. "Honestly, Mom, you spoiled your baby terribly. She's never going to grow up."

"Not if I can help it," Madison agreed with a laugh. "But I won't tease you any more about Seth today. Mom's getting that you're-going-into-time-out-young-lady look."

"And you are, too, if you don't stop harassing your sister," their mother replied with an exaggerated sternness that didn't fool any of them.

Enjoying the rare interlude with her family, despite her younger sister's teasing, Meagan returned to the table and firmly changed the subject. Still, thoughts of her upcoming date with Seth hovered at the back of her mind. She knew she would ask herself later, when she was alone, if she had made a mistake in agreeing to go out with her intriguing neighbor despite her long-standing dating rules.

Chapter Four

On the following Tuesday afternoon, Seth entered his kitchen from the garage, setting down his car keys and sniffing the air appreciatively. "Smells delicious. Spaghetti sauce?"

"The sauce is simmering and the garlic bread's wrapped in foil in the warming oven. Salad's in the fridge. All you have to do is boil the pasta," Nina assured him with a smile as she emerged from the open doorway of the laundry room attached to the kitchen, her arms filled with fluffy towels folded straight from the dryer.

The housekeeper's gray hair was in the usual loose bun at the back of her head, and her chubby figure was encased in dark stretch pants with a loose, floral polyester shirt. Seth had rarely seen her wear any other style. She was in her late sixties, but she looked and acted younger. Though a few pounds overweight and on medication for high blood pressure, she was in pretty good shape overall, bustling around the house with almost endless energy during the hours she worked for him, keeping his household running like a well-oiled machine.

"That sounds delicious. Thanks."

"You're home early."

Because Alice was old enough to be on her own for an hour or so, Nina was usually either already gone or on her way out when Seth arrived home unless they'd arranged for her to stay with Alice when he had plans that kept him out late. Occasionally she ate dinner with him and Alice, but Nina had a busy calendar. Most of her evenings were filled with activities, from bingo to church activities to her bowling league. His sixty-something widowed housekeeper had a much more active social life than he did, Seth thought wryly.

"I had an appointment canceled at the last minute, so I sneaked out while I had the chance. Where's Alice?"

"She's out in the backyard with that hound of hers, trying to teach it tricks. I wish her luck. That mutt's got a head harder than a concrete wall."

Seth chuckled. "He does at that."

Still, even after just one obedience class, he thought he was seeing a little improvement in Waldo's behavior. Or was he being too much of an optimist?

"I'm just going to run these towels upstairs and then I'm done for the day. Unless you want me to cook the pasta for you before I leave? Won't take me but a few minutes."

"No, thanks. I'm perfectly capable of boiling pasta. I know this is your bingo night."

Smiling, Nina left the kitchen, humming some old gospel song under her breath, as she was prone to do. He really was fond of Nina, Seth thought, setting his briefcase on the kitchen table. She was a treasured member of his small family.

He shrugged out of his suit coat, slung it over the back of a chair and opened the fridge. He was thirsty. He'd have a quick sip of the fresh-brewed iced tea Nina always kept on hand, then head upstairs to change before cooking the pasta.

"Hi, Dad." A radiant smile beaming from amidst her wind-tossed curls, Alice burst through the back door into the kitchen. "I've been walking Waldo on the leash. He's doing a lot better. He sits almost every time I tell him to."

"Just keep working with him, he'll get there."

"I know. He really is smart."

"If you say so," he teased, ruffling her already-tousled hair.

"Aw, Dad. You know he—"

A muffled shriek and a heavy thump from another part of the house interrupted Alice's words. Seth set the tea glass down so abruptly that liquid splashed on the counter, but he didn't linger to clean it up. He dashed out of the kitchen toward the foyer stairway.

His heart almost stopped in response to the sight that greeted him there.

Nina lay at the bottom of the stairs, one leg twisted horribly beneath her, her face ashen and damp with the tears streaming from her eyes. "Oh, Seth, I—"

"Don't try to talk," he urged, kneeling beside her and taking her hand. He didn't want to move away from her even long enough to grab a phone. "Alice, call 9-1-1."

Looking shaken, his daughter dashed for the closest telephone. Alice had been trained from an early age how to make emergency calls for help, Seth reminded himself, folding both his hands around Nina's icy one.

"I fell," Nina explained unnecessarily through trembling lips, her voice a choked, pain-ridden whisper. "I'm so sorry."

He couldn't imagine why she was apologizing. He hoped she wasn't going into shock. Frustrated by his sense of almost overwhelming helplessness, he tried to keep his voice calm and soothing. "Just lie still, Nina. Alice is calling an ambulance. We're going to take very good care of you, you hear?"

She closed her eyes. Her hand was so cold and limp in his that it scared him for a minute, but he could hear her ragged breathing. She looked so uncomfortable in the twisted position, but he was terrified to try to move her. What if she had a spinal injury or something? He had very little experience with emergency first aid.

"The ambulance is on the way," Alice reported breathlessly when she returned, her young face bleached of color. "Is she going to be okay, Daddy?"

"She'll be fine," he said firmly, hoping to reassure Alice and Nina—and himself, as well.

Nina groaned softly without opening her eyes. He wasn't even sure she'd heard him.

The doorbell rang only a couple of minutes later. It seemed too soon for the ambulance to have arrived, he thought with a frown. Nor had he heard a siren.

Alice rushed to open the door. "Meagan," Seth heard her say, to his surprise. "Nina's over here, at the foot of the stairs."

He felt the frown he was already wearing deepen. Alice had called Meagan? He wasn't sure why. They needed paramedics, not a friendly neighbor.

Looking more composed than any of them, Meagan knelt at Nina's other side, giving Seth a little nod of greeting as she did so. Leaning over the housekeeper, she spoke quietly, her voice reassuringly steady. "Nina? Can you hear me?"

Her eyes still closed, Nina whispered, "Yes."

Doing a quick visual assessment of the housekeeper's position, Meagan asked, "Will you open your eyes for me?"

Maybe Meagan had dealt with this sort of thing before, Seth thought, finding some measure of comfort in her composure. She seemed to have some idea of what she was doing—which was more than he could say for himself.

"I hurt." Nina's broken whimper was heartbreaking. Seth squeezed her hand gently again, wanting to remind her that he was there for her.

Though her expression held sympathy, Meagan continued to speak firmly. "I know you do, but I'd like you to open your eyes for just a minute. Did you hit your head?"

Her face pinched and dazed, Nina responded to the resolute tone. Still clinging to Seth, she squinted up at Meagan. "I—I don't think so. My leg."

Meagan held Nina's other wrist now, her fingers placed purposefully on the older woman's pulse. Definitely knew what she was doing, Seth concluded, rapidly adjusting his previous impressions of her. For some reason he couldn't explain, he'd thought of her as an office worker at the hospital. Now he guessed RN. It seemed odd now that they'd never talked about her work.

"Yes, I can see you've broken your right leg." Meagan ran a hand lightly down Nina's side and hip, her fingertips skimming the twisted leg through the fabric stretched over it. "Lie very still and I'll try to ease you into a little more comfortable position while we wait for the ambulance, okay? I don't want to move you much, but it must hurt twisted under you this way."

"Uh—should you move her at all?" Seth asked in concern. "I mean—"

Meagan gave him a rather quizzical look, but replied lightly, "I'm only going to shift her position a very little. It will take some of the pressure off her hip and knee and maybe ease her discomfort a little. Let her keep holding your hand. Do you understand, Nina? Squeeze Seth's hand if you need to. I don't want you to try to move at all, just let me make the adjustments. Tell me if I do anything at all that causes you more pain."

Biting back another protest, Seth watched as Meagan carefully and competently eased the older woman into a somewhat less twisted position. And then he blinked in bemusement when she drew a stethoscope out of the canvas bag she'd set on the floor when she'd knelt down. He'd thought it was a purse.

"Does your blood pressure normally run high, Nina?"

"Y-yes. A little."

"All right. Try to breath naturally. I hear the ambulance approaching. You'll be at the hospital soon and we can get you all patched up. You're going to be fine, okay?"

"Thank you, Dr. Baker," Nina whispered. She had always called her Meagan within Seth's hearing before, obviously on invitation to do so, but she seemed to take comfort from the more formal title now.

"You're welcome."

Seth glanced at Alice, who crouched nearby, rocking slightly to calm herself as they waited for help. She didn't look at all surprised to hear Nina call Meagan doctor. Apparently, he was the only one who hadn't known.

The wail of the distant, but approaching siren was growing louder when he regained his voice. "You're a doctor," he said rather stupidly, his mind reeling from the series of shocks.

Glancing up from her ongoing examination of his injured housekeeper, Meagan returned his look with a slight frown of confusion. "I'm a surgeon. I thought—surely you knew that?"

"No, I—" He pushed a hand through his hair, trying to get a grip on his rattled emotions. "I didn't know. Alice told me you worked at RCMC, but I thought—well, I guess I assumed you worked in the administrative offices."

"Oh."

He couldn't tell from either her tone or her expression whether she was insulted by his assumption. Had it been a sexist conjecture on his part? He didn't believe that. He had simply misinterpreted the few bits of information he'd been given about her. Apparently his daughter had known Meagan was a doctor, since she'd called her to come assist Nina. He could think of no reason for Alice to deliberately withhold the information, so she must have assumed, like Meagan, that he had already known somehow.

He was hazily aware that his perception of Meagan had just shifted, but he didn't allow himself to analyze the change just then. He had to make sure Nina was tended to, and he heard the ambulance pulling into the driveway at that moment. Alice had the front door open and was out on the porch, waving frantically at the paramedics.

After greeting the EMTs—both of whom seemed to recognize her, Seth realized—Meagan pulled Seth aside while the medics stabilized their patient for the ride to the hospital.

"I'll ride in the ambulance with Nina," Meagan offered. "She seems to be doing fairly well, but I'm a little concerned about her blood pressure. I'm sure she'll be fine," she added quickly in response to whatever she saw in his expression. "And these guys certainly know what they're doing. I just want to monitor her during the ride."

He nodded. "Alice and I will follow in my car."

"Drive safely," she warned him. "It will take a while for her to be processed and admitted. I'll find you in the emergency waiting room as soon as I have news for you. Is there someone you should call for her? A family member?"

"Her daughter lives in Mississippi. I'll call her now. Nina doesn't have any other family in this area that I'm aware of."

"Her purse!" Alice dashed out of the entryway, returning moments later with a big, red leather bag. "I bet her insurance cards and everything are in here."

"Good thinking, Alice. We'll need those."

A little color returned to his daughter's pale cheeks in response to Meagan's praise, Seth noted before he turned to Meagan again. "Get her the best help available," he urged. "Don't worry about costs, we'll take care of that."

Meagan nodded. "Don't worry, Nina will get the best of care."

"We're going to move her to the gurney, Dr. Baker," one of the paramedics announced, having secured the housekeeper to a backboard.

Slinging the strap of Nina's bag over her shoulder and tucking her own beneath the same arm, Meagan nodded and moved toward them, patting Alice's shoulder with her free hand as she passed the girl. "You've been very helpful, Alice. I'm proud of you for staying so calm."

"I don't feel calm," Alice said to Seth, leaning against him for a moment. "I'm so scared for Nina."

He wrapped his arms around her in a bracing hug, needing the contact, himself. "Me, too, honey. But she's getting help now. She'll be okay."

Alice nodded against his chest. "Meagan will take care of her."

"Yes," Seth murmured, watching Meagan follow the

others out the front door toward the waiting ambulance. "She will."

He had a lot to do in the next few minutes, he reminded himself, sending Alice to quickly fetch whatever she wanted to take to the hospital to pass the time while they sat in the waiting room. He still wore the dress shirt and suit pants he'd had on earlier, but he didn't want to take time to change. He loosened the top buttons of his shirt and turned back the sleeves as he hurried into the kitchen.

Hastily, he stashed away the food Nina had prepared for them, swallowing hard in response to the painful awareness that this would be the last meal she would cook for them at least for the foreseeable future. And then he picked up his phone and located the contact number for Nina's daughter Lisa, written in the back of the calendar by his always-prepared housekeeper. He knew Lisa would want to be notified immediately, and would probably be on her way to Little Rock as soon as she could make travel arrangements.

There wasn't time to think about Meagan now. About why he'd assumed she was an office worker, and why he'd been so stunned to find out she wasn't. Once he was certain Nina would be all right, then he would take time to ask himself why he was so shaken to discover that Meagan was a surgeon, and not the efficient clerical worker he'd naively envisioned.

Almost an hour after Nina had been wheeled into the hospital, Meagan joined Seth and Alice in the emergency department waiting area. They looked tired and worried. The expressions were familiar to her; she saw them all the time on the faces of her patients' family members. She responded by switching automatically into doctor mode, keeping her voice soothing and professional.

"She's stable and resting fairly comfortably now. She's

been given something for pain so she's drifting in and out, but when she's awake she's coherent. Her leg is broken in two places: the femur, just above the knee, and the tibia, just below the knee. Fortunately, the knee itself looks good. She'll have to have surgery to repair the breaks. She's scheduled for tomorrow morning."

Seth nodded grimly. He motioned with the cell phone he held in his right hand. "I just talked to her daughter again. She and her husband are on their way. They should be here in another two and a half hours or so."

"Are you going to operate on Nina, Meagan?" Alice asked.

"No, sweetie, I'm a general surgeon, not an orthopedic surgeon. But I know who's going to do the surgery, and he's very good, okay? He'd be the one I'd choose if it were my own mother needing the operation."

"Can we see her?"

"She's being moved to a room for the night. You can see her as soon as they get her settled in."

Alice nodded reluctantly.

"Have you had dinner?"

Alice's lip quivered a little. "Nina was making spaghetti sauce."

The girl had been so brave until this point. Meagan suspected reaction was just setting in. She glanced at her watch. "The hospital cafeteria is open for another half hour, or the café off the lobby serves sandwiches, salads and desserts round the clock. Why don't you two get something to eat and I'll let you know as soon as Nina's in her room."

"Would you like to join us for a meal?" Seth asked, resting a hand on Alice's shoulder as if he, too, was aware that his daughter needed a little extra reassurance. "You're probably hungry, too."

"I'll go check on Nina again, and then I'll find you."

He nodded. "We'll be in the café. I think sandwiches and salads are all either of us want tonight."

"All right." She smiled at Alice. "Just a tip—the chocolate cake is amazing."

She was pleased when Alice returned the smile, though a bit weakly. "I do like chocolate cake."

"Then let's go get you some," her dad said promptly, giving Meagan a quick look of gratitude. "After the sandwich."

"I know, Daddy."

Meagan smiled as she turned to return to Nina.

It was after ten by the time Seth drove Meagan home from the hospital that evening. Because she'd ridden in the ambulance, Meagan didn't have her car, but she could have called Madison to come get her. She even offered to have Madison take her and Alice home earlier because it was a school night, but Alice didn't want to leave the hospital until her father did. Seth had been reluctant to leave before Nina's daughter arrived. Meagan suspected he felt responsible in some way for Nina's accident, though surely he knew he had in no way caused her to fall.

Seth assured her they'd be fine, but Meagan had opted to stay to help keep Alice entertained and distracted from her distress. She knew seeing Nina crumpled at the foot of the stairs had been a traumatic experience for the girl, even though Alice had handled it very well.

Exhausted, Alice fell asleep in the backseat before Seth had driven a mile from the hospital. Restrained by the shoulder belt, she slept with her head lolling against the padded headrest behind her. She didn't even stir when Seth parked in Meagan's driveway and got out to walk her to the door.

"I'll have to shake her awake when we get home," Seth

said with a chuckle as they glanced back at the car. "She's getting a little too old for me to carry her inside and tuck her in without waking her."

"Will she be okay for school tomorrow?"

"Yeah. A little sleepy, maybe, but she'll be fine."

"Nina's daughter seemed nice. She's eager to move Nina to Mississippi to live with her, isn't she?"

"Yeah, she's wanted Nina to move there for the past year or so. I wouldn't be surprised if she'll get her wish now. It's going to be a while before Nina's back up to full speed."

"Nina's in good health. She'll make a full recovery, though you're right, it will be several weeks before she's completely healed."

"Lisa will still make every effort to convince Nina to stay in Mississippi with her. Which means I'll have to hire a new housekeeper, I guess. Alice is old enough to stay by herself for a couple hours after school, but I don't really want her staying home by herself all summer. And even though she's old enough to do quite a few things around the house, I think it best if we have some help."

"You'll miss Nina."

"Yes, I will. She's been with me for several years. I always knew I could count on her for whatever I needed from her."

"I've only known her a couple of weeks, of course, but I like her very much."

"I know she appreciates everything you did for her today. We all do. Thank you for rushing over. I didn't even realize Alice had called you."

And of course Seth hadn't called her, himself, because he hadn't even known she was a doctor. Meagan still found it startling that he had been unaware of that fact. They hadn't spent much time together, of course, and had rarely been alone. Their few conversations had focused on Alice, for the most part. She had mentioned she was on a medical leave, but she supposed she hadn't said from what. But it did seem odd that neither Alice nor Nina had mentioned Meagan's job to Seth. She guessed they didn't really think of her in her career much because they had seen her only at home on leave.

Funny, so many people asked almost immediately what she did for a living when meeting her for the first time. She hadn't gone into medicine to impress anyone, but because she enjoyed the work and the challenges involved but still some people treated her with a bit more deference once they learned what she did. Would Seth act any differently toward her now that he knew she wasn't the office worker he'd thought, for some reason? She couldn't imagine why he would.

"I'm glad I could help, and I didn't mind at all that Alice called," she assured him. "She's welcome to come here after school while you look for a replacement for Nina. I'm not cleared to return to work for another couple of weeks, so I'll be here, and I would enjoy her company."

"I'll tell her. I know she enjoys visiting with you. Just feel free to send her home when you get tired or have anything else to do."

"Of course."

"So, um—we're still on for that charity thing Friday evening?"

"Sure." That was an odd thing for him to ask, she thought, studying his face in the yellowish porch lighting. "*You* still want to go, right?"

"Yeah. I mean, Lisa's here to take care of Nina, and I'm sort of expected to show up..." Apparently realizing he sounded less than gracious, he paused, then finished smoothly, "And I'm looking forward to spending the evening with you, of course."

She smiled and started to respond lightly, but was interrupted by the buzz of her cell phone. Frowning, she drew it from her pocket and glanced at the screen. "It's my mother. It's later than she usually calls."

"I hope everything's okay."

She held the phone to her ear. "Mom?"

Seth hovered nearby, looking torn between giving her privacy and wanting to be there for her if she needed anything.

"I know it's late, but do you feel up to coming over, Meagan? I don't like the way your grandmother is breathing. Maybe it's nothing, but she seems to be struggling a little. I'd feel better if you look at her. I tried Mitch, but he's on call tonight. I was told he's in an emergency surgery. If you don't feel up to coming, I can try Maddie. I don't want to call for an ambulance if I'm just over-reacting."

What else could go wrong that day? Meagan pushed a hand through her hair, feeling her still-recovering energy waning. "I'll be there in fifteen minutes. Stay calm, Mom, we'll take care of her, okay?"

"All right. You're sure you feel like driving?"

"Of course I do. It's only a few miles. Don't worry about me, just take care of Meemaw until I get there."

She hung up the phone and slipped it back into her pocket, already opening her purse to find her car keys as she spoke to Seth. "My grandmother's in poor health and Mom wants me to come check on her. It's probably nothing serious, but Mom will feel better if I look in on her."

"Is there anything you need? Are you okay to drive? I could take you."

She smiled, grateful for the offer, though she shook her head. "Thank you, but I'm fine. Trust me, I'm used to being called out late at night."

"I see. The doctor's life, huh?"

"Pretty much," she said, keys in hand now. "My life is much more hectic than this when I'm not on leave."

"I'm sure it is."

Something in his tone made her frown a little, but she didn't have time to analyze it. "Good night, Seth. Let me know if you and Alice need anything. And tell her to feel free to come by after school tomorrow."

He was already backing toward his car. "I hope your grandmother is okay. Let me know if there's anything *I* can do for *you*."

Meagan glanced into her rearview mirror as she drove away minutes later. Seth had already driven into his garage and closed the door, she noted. She pictured him guiding his sleepy daughter into the house. And then she made an effort to put that sweet little vignette out of her mind and concentrate on her own family's needs.

Early Wednesday afternoon, Meagan was just finishing a call with one of her partners, catching up on office business, when she was interrupted by the beep of an incoming call. Seth. She and her partner said their goodbyes and she picked up the other call.

"How's your grandmother?" he asked.

"A little better today. Thank you for asking."

"So she wasn't having a crisis when you had to rush over there last night?"

"Nothing serious, this time. She was developing a respiratory infection, which is fairly common for her these days. Her immune system is depressed by her illnesses and her other medications, which makes her highly susceptible to infection. I put her on a round of antibiotics for ten days. We'll watch her closely, but I think she'll recover fairly easily."

This time, she repeated silently. The day was approaching all too quickly when antibiotics would not be enough.

"How's Nina?" she asked, pushing that all-too-familiar awareness to the back of her mind. She knew Seth would be closely monitoring Nina's progress.

"She came through the surgery just fine. I sat with Lisa and Alan during the operation and I got to see Nina for a few minutes before I left for the office. Her blood pressure is still a little too high, but she should be able to leave the hospital in a few days. Lisa let me know that she intends to keep Nina with her in Mississippi, even after she's back on her feet. She and Alan have a garage studio they're converting for Nina's use, so she'll have her independence but will still be close to them."

"I know you'll miss her, but it's nice that Nina will be close to her daughter."

"Yeah, I guess," he said without much enthusiasm. "I don't suppose you know anyone looking for a full-time housekeeping job?"

"No, I'm afraid not. I have someone who comes in to do the heavy cleaning twice a month, but she prefers part-time work. She wouldn't be interested in a full-time position. I'll ask around for you, if you like."

"Well, if you hear of anyone, I'd appreciate the tip."

"How was Alice this morning?"

"Fine, once I convinced her Nina's going to be okay. I don't mind admitting that whole episode scared the bejeebers out of both of us."

She smiled a little in response to his wording. "I'm sure it did. I was relieved when I first saw Nina and realized there were no head or internal injuries."

"Alice wanted to go with me to the hospital today, but I convinced her to go on to school. She felt better about it when I told her she could come to your house after school.

That invitation is still open, isn't it? You don't have any other plans?"

"Of course she's welcome. Do you need me to pick her up?"

"No, thanks, that's not necessary. Alice's best friend's grandmother Margaret will chauffeur the kids both ways. She won't even let me reimburse her for gas."

"That's very generous of her."

"She's fond of Alice. And of Nina. They met for coffee occasionally. She said she's going to stop by the hospital on the way to pick up the girls this afternoon."

Meagan heard a woman's voice in the background of Seth's call—a secretary, she guessed—and then Seth's muffled reply before he returned his attention to her. "I'm sorry, Meagan, I have to go. Send Alice home if you need to leave or anything, okay? She'll be fine on her own until I get there."

"Don't worry about her, Seth. We'll be fine."

"Okay. Well, then…I'll see you."

"See you." She realized she was smiling when she disconnected the call, and she suspected her sister would have teased her mercilessly had Madison seen that particular smile. Madison would probably say something silly—like calling Meagan smitten or infatuated by Alice's cute dad. As the smile slowly faded, Meagan had an uneasy suspicion that Madison's imagined accusation wouldn't have been completely wrong.

Chapter Five

"Wow." Having seen Meagan only in casual clothing until that moment, Seth was suitably impressed when she opened the door to him in more formal attire Friday evening. "You look very nice."

That was most definitely an understatement. On some blondes, the long, basic black sheath might have been too stark or too bland. Neither was true for Meagan. The dress fit her well-toned curves to perfection. The draped neckline dipped low enough to expose an appealing glimpse of creamy skin accented with a glitter of diamond pendant. Seth had to make a masterful effort to keep his gaze on her face rather than her cleavage or the length of leg revealed by a thigh-high slit in the straight skirt. He supposed the dress was modest enough by most standards, but he still felt his blood pressure rise a bit in response to what it revealed.

She smiled in pleasure at the compliment. "Thank you.

It's been a while since I've had an occasion to dress up. You look very dashing in your tux, too."

He dipped into a teasing bow. "Why, thank you, ma'am."

Tucking a shiny little black clutch bag beneath her arm, she locked her door and walked with him to his car. He opened her door for her, waited until she was safely tucked inside, then closed the door and rounded the front of the vehicle. It felt good to perform those little rituals, he realized with a faint smile.

He loved being a dad. For a while, he'd even enjoyed being a husband. Tonight, it was kind of fun to remember what it felt like to be just a single guy on a date with an attractive woman who made his pulse race.

"How's your grandmother?" he asked as soon as they were on the road toward the downtown hotel where the event was being held.

"She's doing as well as can be expected, thank you."

"How's your mother holding up?"

"Being my grandmother's primary caregiver is tough on her, but she insists on doing most of it herself. She's handling it all pretty well, though."

He heard the concern underlying her words, and figured she worried almost as much about her mother as she did her grandmother. "Alice said she met your mom at your house yesterday after school."

Meagan smiled wryly. "With all mom's other responsibilities, she still thinks she needs to bring casseroles for me to stash in my freezer during my recuperation. Even though I keep telling her I'm perfectly capable of cooking for myself now. I really wasn't down long, though to hear Mother talk about it, you'd think I'd been at death's door."

He still wasn't sure exactly what type of surgery Meagan

had undergone, but that seemed too personal to ask. Instead, he commented, "Alice liked your mother. She said she was funny."

"Mom liked Alice, too. They got into a spirited discussion about a science fiction program on TV they both follow."

"Ah. The one about the crazy town with all the oddball geniuses? Alice is obsessed with that show."

"So is Mom, apparently. She watches quite a bit of television when she isn't reading, since taking care of my grandmother keeps her at home most evenings."

"How long ago did you lose your father?"

"A little over five years ago. I remember Alice mentioned that your father is still living. In…Texas?"

"Dallas," he confirmed with a nod.

"Are you close?"

He shrugged. "We get along okay but I wouldn't call us close, especially since my mother died ten years ago. He's an architect and he travels a lot with his job, always has. We see each other a few times a year, talk on the phone once a month or so. Alice emails him occasionally and sends him pictures of herself."

"I see."

From the corner of his eye, he saw her toying with the little tassel hanging from her clutch zipper. Was she a bit more nervous about this outing than her serene expression let on? He had to admit it felt a bit different being with her without Alice chattering between them.

After a momentary pause, she spoke again. "Alice was looking forward to her sleepover party this evening."

"Yes. Her three best friends are all going to be there. There will be some major giggling in that house tonight."

Meagan laughed softly. "If it's anything like the

sleepover parties I attended at her age, I'm sure you're right. I hope she'll get a few hours sleep."

He shrugged. "She can rest tomorrow. She doesn't have any other plans, except for Waldo's obedience class."

"What are you going to do about Waldo's class next week? Alice mentioned that next weekend is her visit with her grandparents in Heber Springs. Will you be taking Waldo to class?"

"I guess so, though the instructors recommend having the same person work with the dog in each class. But he's just going to have to settle for me this time. If he flunks that class, Alice can blame me rather than her precious dog."

She smiled in response to the joke, but spoke seriously. "It's nice that Alice's grandparents live close enough for her to maintain a relationship with them, especially since her mother is so far away."

Seth nodded. "It's just under a two-hour drive to their home on Greer's Ferry Lake. They moved to Heber Springs when Harold—Alice's grandfather—retired from his law practice in Jonesboro, where they raised Colleen. I met Colleen in law school, here in Little Rock. Her parents are decent people. They've mellowed in the past few years, and they're very fond of their grandchildren. They fly to Denver fairly often to visit their other daughter's family, and they see Alice one weekend a month. She enjoys spending time with them."

"I've always been close to my grandparents. My father's parents are still living in Florida, and my paternal grandmother and I stay in touch through the computer. She's addicted to the social networking sites. My mom's mother, on the other hand, has never touched a computer. She always considered them vaguely sinister."

Seth laughed. "There are times I'd agree with her."

Traffic had almost stopped when they approached the parking deck of the luxury hotel. He inched the car forward, hoping the deck wouldn't fill up before he found a space. At least Meagan seemed to have relaxed with him a little during their chat about Alice. He wasn't sure why she'd been tense at the beginning. Maybe it was just that first date thing.

Ten minutes later, they walked into the glittering ballroom. DeAnna had gone all out on decorations for the event, which was to raise money for a local battered women's shelter. He'd never seen so much glittering purple in one venue. Attendance was good; the ballroom was almost filled with attendees in elegant clothing, their conversations underscored by the music of the eight-member orchestra situated in a far corner of the room.

He spotted quite a few familiar faces immediately, mingling in ever-changing groups or seated at the purple-and-silver draped tables arranged around the edges of the ballroom. He smiled and nodded toward one of the portly senior partners of the law firm, who was making a beeline toward the food tables. On the other side of the large room guests mingled around more tables, some scribbling their names on pads flanked by elegant floral arrangements. A silent auction was part of the night's festivities. Seth supposed he'd have to examine the offerings and make a bid, himself. He hoped there was something worth bidding for.

"Dr. Baker!"

Both Seth and Meagan turned in response to the greeting. A heavyset matron in a dress better suited to a somewhat younger woman surged toward them, towing a painfully thin man in an ill-fitting tuxedo behind her.

Glancing at Meagan, Seth could almost see her groping for a name. "Mrs., um, Clayton, isn't it?"

"Clanton," the woman corrected. "Olivia Clanton. You took out my gallbladder last fall?"

"Yes, of course," Meagan said smoothly, smiling graciously at the couple. "How are you?"

"Well, I haven't had any more trouble with my gallbladder, of course," the woman replied with a laugh. "But I've been plagued with pain in my left shoulder something fierce. Do you think surgery would help it?"

"You should see your primary care physician, who will refer you to someone who specializes in whatever is causing your problem. An orthopedist or rheumatologist, perhaps."

Not particularly satisfied with Meagan's subtle brush-off, the woman went into more detail about the pain she encountered whenever she raised her left arm above her head. Her husband stood behind her, giving both Meagan and Seth wryly apologetic looks. Seemingly from experience, Meagan was able to extricate herself fairly quickly. Claiming to see someone else trying to catch her attention, she excused herself and nudged Seth in the opposite direction. He complied happily, leading her toward the silent auction tables.

"I guess you get hit up all the time for free medical advice," he commented sympathetically.

She shrugged lightly. "Probably no more than you get hit up for free legal advice."

He nodded to concede her point.

It turned out both of them knew quite a few people at the event. Considering they had a few mutual friends in the local professional community, it was actually rather surprising they hadn't met previously. She introduced him to a few people, and he did the same for her. It didn't escape his notice that people reacted somewhat differently when he added "doctor" to the front of her name.

She seemed quite comfortable making small talk with strangers, sharing air kisses with acquaintances, skillfully juggling champagne and hors d'oeuvres, politely applauding the trite speeches from the event organizers. He couldn't help remembering how Colleen had thrived on this sort of occasion. If it had been up to her, they'd have attended some sort of social event almost every evening of the week. Networking was important to their careers, she had lectured repeatedly. They had to place themselves repeatedly in front of the social elite to be accepted as one of them.

That had been one of the issues that had caused the most friction between them. Seth had wanted to spend more evenings at home with Alice. He hadn't been opposed to attending even one function a week, but more than that was too much for him. Eventually Colleen had started attending without him, though she never left without a complaint that her husband refused to support her career aspirations. He'd always considered that an unfair accusation. He'd done everything he could to support her, but he would not miss his daughter's childhood to further Colleen's ambition.

Out of the corner of his eye, he watched Meagan chatting and laughing with an acquaintance beside the silent auction tables while he tried to pay attention to the smug boasting of a couple of the law firm's most prestigious clients. She seemed to be enjoying herself. He supposed she was glad to be out and about again, but he couldn't help wondering if this was her idea of a good time.

Seth wasn't much of a dancer, despite the classes Colleen had forced him to attend early in their marriage. She had insisted that learning to dance and to play golf and tennis were all crucial for anyone with aspirations of mingling with the professional and social elite. Still, he didn't mind so much dancing with Meagan a couple of times during that evening. She was very relaxed about it, which put him more at ease and he had to admit she fit very nicely into his arms. Those few turns around the small dance floor were unexpectedly turning out to be his favorite part of the evening.

Meagan was just full of surprises, he thought as they ended another pleasant dance and politely applauded the orchestra. The more he learned about her, the more he wanted to know. It seemed she was bewitching him as easily as she had his daughter. He couldn't help worrying a little about the potential complications—for all of them.

Meagan was secretly relieved when Seth hinted he was ready to leave the charity gala somewhat early. He'd told her on the way in that he didn't tend to stay until the end of a party, and she'd assured him that wasn't her usual habit either. Usually, she'd added, she had to get away early because she would have to be at the hospital only a few hours afterward. Even though that wasn't the case this time, she was still ready to leave as soon as Seth indicated they'd stayed long enough for his purposes.

All in all, it hadn't been a bad evening. Seth was certainly a pleasant escort. The fundraiser had been for a good cause. She'd seen the social politics at work, of course; that was part of any society event. Plenty of kissing up and schmoozing, but that was as common in the medical world as in the legal or financial or other professions. She'd never been particularly interested in playing those games, settling instead for doing just what was expected to keep her active in her own professional network.

She'd concluded long ago that she would never have been happy with a socialite's life, serving to bolster her spouse's career or flitting from one charity event to another. She was so impatient to get back to her own work, to feel truly useful again. There had been parts of her enforced vacation she'd enjoyed, she thought with a glance from beneath her lashes at Seth, but she was glad there was only one week remaining before she could get back to the hospital.

Squirming a little in her seat, she felt her healing abdomen muscles protest the movement. She was frustrated by how quickly she still tired after her surgery. She was accustomed to going at top speed for long hours without feeling the effects until she crashed at home at the end of the day, to being on her feet twelve or fourteen hours a day without even being aware of the passing time. Now, after three hours at a standard charity function, she felt as though she'd just run a daylong marathon.

"How are you holding up?" Seth asked as he drove, suggesting he was not oblivious to the signs of her weariness, even though his eyes were focused on the road ahead.

She made an attempt to speak briskly. "I'm fine, thanks. Your partner's wife put together quite an affair, didn't she?"

"Yeah, she did a good job. I'm sure she had plenty of help, but still she can be proud of the results. She raised a tidy amount of cash for the shelter tonight."

"Yes, she did. I know the donation will be greatly appreciated. My sister volunteers at that shelter sometimes, and they always need extra funds."

"What does your sister do?"

"My sister's a second-year resident in the psychiatry program. Mom works part time as a bookkeeper and serves as full-time caregiver for my grandmother. She needs the spa day worse than any of us."

"Your sister is also a doctor?"

She nodded. "My brother, too. I tease them about following in my footsteps."

"Three doctors in the family. Your mother must be proud."

"Our parents just wanted us to be self-sufficient. Mom would be proud no matter what careers we had chosen to accomplish that goal."

"That's what I want for Alice," he confided. "For her to be happy and secure in her future. I want her to be prepared to take care of herself."

"An important goal for any child, boy or girl," she agreed. "My parents encouraged us to train for a career that would always be in demand, preferably one we enjoyed doing. They didn't push medical school, but they approved our choices."

"What sort of medicine does your brother practice?"

"He's a surgeon, too. Pediatric orthopedics. He's in the last year of his residency."

"And you all plan to remain here in Arkansas?"

"Yes. Mitch considered going elsewhere for his residency, but our dad died just before Mitch's last year of medical school. Our grandmother had just had her first small stroke. Mitch felt like he should stay close to Mom, even though she tried to convince him she would be fine if he wanted to leave the state for a few years. Arkansas was always Madison's first choice. She loves being near to the family."

"Nice that you're all so close-knit."

She smiled a little wistfully. "Yes, it is. Even though the careers we've chosen have limited our time together. As I said, it's rare for us all to have a day to spend together. I hardly remember the last Christmas when at least one of us wasn't working or on call. But we all call or see Mom as often as we can, and she keeps us informed on how everyone is doing and we get together when we can."

Seth responded only with a nod as he merged into traffic

on the highway toward their neighborhood. He seemed to be growing more distracted as they neared her house, for some reason.

He had just taken the exit from the freeway when he asked, "Do you go to a lot of those charity things?"

She shrugged. "My share, I guess. Usually for some sort of medical cause—funding research for various diseases or raising money for new hospital equipment, that sort of thing. Why?"

"Just curious. Do you like them?"

Was he asking if she'd enjoyed the evening? She worded her response carefully. "I always try to have a nice time."

"I don't go to many. I have a few pet charities I try to support. There's no way to keep up with all the good causes. And I attend a few, like tonight, because there's no politically acceptable way to get out of it without offending someone important to my job. I mean, it was a good cause but I'd have been just as happy to send a check as to attend the gala, you know?"

If there was a message imbedded in that speech, she seemed to be missing it. "I'm sure a lot of people there felt that way tonight, though everyone seemed to be on good behavior."

He nodded. "Just saying."

Fortunately, he turned into her driveway just then, so she didn't have time to come up with a response. Which was good, because she wasn't at all sure what, if anything, he expected her to say.

She wasn't surprised that he insisted on walking her to her door, nor did she protest. She appreciated the little niceties of dating as much as any woman.

"Thank you for going with me tonight," he said as she stuck her key in the lock. "I enjoyed your company."

Her hand on the doorknob, she smiled up at him. "I had a very nice time."

He hesitated a moment, as though he were reluctant to leave. Knowing he was returning to an empty house, she wondered if he was hoping she would invite him in.

"I usually have a cup of tea to relax after one of these things," she said somewhat tentatively. "Would you like to have a cup with me before you head home?"

She was satisfied that she'd worded the invitation clearly enough. Just a cup of tea and a few more minutes of conversation and then she'd expect him to be on his way. Considering they were still in the process of getting to know each other, she was far from ready for anything more, regardless of the attraction simmering between them.

His pause was almost imperceptible. She suspected he'd analyzed her words and her tone before responding, "Tea sounds nice."

Refusing to second-guess the impulse, she opened the door and ushered him in. Aware that this was his first time inside her home, she watched him glance around as she set her purse and keys on an entryway table. She wondered if he noticed that her decorating style was actually quite similar to his own. Clean, modern lines; inviting, conversational groupings; warm, earthy colors. He favored darker wood tones than she did, but other than that their styles meshed quite well. So, she wasn't surprised when he said, "I like your place."

"Thank you. I usually drink my tea at the kitchen table, but we can sit in here if you'd rather."

"The kitchen works for me," he answered promptly. "You might have noticed, I tend to prefer casualness to formality."

"I have noticed," she said with a smile as he tugged at

his bowtie, letting it hang at the sides of his now-unfastened collar. "You can't get out of that tux fast enough, can you?"

Okay, so that question hadn't been worded so well. What had been intended as a teasing acknowledgement of his discomfort had instead led her thoughts onto paths they really had no business being on at this point. Firmly pushing thoughts of Seth-sans-tux from her mind, she asked quickly, "What kind of tea do you prefer? I have quite a few selections."

Looking at her just a little quizzically—oh, heavens, was she blushing? At her age? Honestly!—he replied, "Earl Grey. Hot."

She had already turned toward the kitchen to hide her pink cheeks, but his words made her spin around again in pleasure, momentary embarrassment forgotten. "I'll make it so, Captain."

A grin spread across his face, making her swallow hard again. Wow. Did this man have a nice smile!

"You're a Trekkie?" he asked in amused disbelief.

"In my family, there's little choice." She turned toward the kitchen again, hearing him follow when she left the living room. "My parents met at a sci-fi convention in the '70s. They had both watched the original series as kids, and they made sure we saw all the series and films."

He laughed. "You're kidding! A sci-fi convention?"

She nodded, accustomed to the reaction to her description of her parents' meeting. "My mom was there on a date with her geeky boyfriend, as she describes him. Dad was dressed as a Klingon. Apparently it was love at first grunt."

Dropping into a chair at the round, glass-topped table in her modern granite and stainless kitchen, Seth grinned. "What about the geeky boyfriend?"

"He met a busty Amazon warrior woman at the same convention, so everyone left happy."

"No wonder Alice was so taken with your mom. Alice loves sci-fi, too." Looking bemused, Seth propped his chin on his fist and watched her fill two clear glass tea mugs from an instant-hot-water dispenser, one of her must-have kitchen conveniences.

"Milk or sugar?" she asked.

"No, thanks. Just tea. You must have had a fun childhood."

She removed two canisters of tea from a cabinet, Earl Grey for Seth, an herbal blend for herself. "I did, actually. Dad was a physics professor at UALR, kind of an oddball but beloved by his students. He stressed the equal values of advanced education, independent self-reliance and quality science fiction as we grew up. He was also obsessed with roller coasters, so we spent a lot of time at amusement parks. Mom's a CPA, and she worked full time for a big Little Rock accounting firm until Dad died and she became responsible for her mother. She was almost always home by four in the afternoons to welcome us home from school."

"Unconventional."

"Yes. But wonderful." Smiling nostalgically, she carried the steaming mugs to the table.

"No wonder you all turned out so well."

"Did you have a happy childhood?"

"It wasn't a bad childhood. Nothing like yours."

"You were an only child," she remembered.

"Yeah. And both my parents were workaholics who focused on their careers almost to the exclusion of anything else. They hated amusement parks. Occasionally they paid a nanny to take me to one, but they'd never have visited one themselves. Said they didn't have time. My earliest childhood memories are of watching them rushing around the house in the mornings, shoving bagels in their mouths while they gathered papers and briefcases and put on their suit jackets."

Seeing her expression, he shook his head. "Don't look so pitying. I had a good childhood. My parents loved me, though they wouldn't have known how to play with me even if they'd had time. That was something I always wanted to change for Alice. I wanted her to remember playtime with me, even though I've made it clear that my work is important, too."

He took a tentative sip of his hot tea. "Colleen's more like my parents. Your sister the psychiatrist would probably have something to say about my ex-wife being very much like my mother, but we'll let that slide for now. Anyway, she loves Alice very much and lets her know it, but she's clueless when it comes to playing or relaxing or anything but work. They'll spend their time in Europe visiting museums and historic landmarks. And Colleen will have the nanny take Alice on the more frivolous adventures while Colleen is in meetings."

"And you won't relax until Alice is safely back home with you," she predicted over the rim of her mug.

He made a face. "Not for a minute."

"How's your search for a new housekeeper going?"

Seth heaved a heavy breath. "I'm trying to find time to interview a few. I've received several resumes, but I've got another crazy week ahead at work. Tomorrow would have been a good day to talk to people, with Alice at her grandparents and all, but I've been called in for a partners' meeting tomorrow that's going to take most of the afternoon. Maybe I can schedule some evening interviews later in the week, or next weekend. Unless…"

Something about his suddenly speculative expression gave her pause. "Unless…?" she repeated.

"Well, you did say you're bored."

She set down her mug. "You're suggesting I interview housekeepers for you?"

His crooked, slightly sheepish smile made her heart trip over a beat. She wasn't sure she could say no to anything in response to that smile. And wasn't *that* a worrisome realization?

"Forget it." His charming smile fading, Seth made a dismissive gesture with one hand, seeming to rethink his impulsive suggestion. "That was too much to ask. Just an impulse…you've done enough for our family already."

"No, just a sec." Now that she wasn't dazzled by his smile, she could think a bit more clearly. "It's not a terrible idea. You're frantically busy, especially since you don't have any help at home just now, and I'm going crazy sitting here with nothing to do. I wouldn't feel comfortable hiring anyone, but I could weed out some of the more obviously unsuitable applicants and make a few recommendations for you."

"Wow, that would be so… But no, really. Interviewing applicants is hardly fun. You should be enjoying your time off."

"I've sat by the pool until I'm sick of my own backyard, and I've read every book I've bought during the past year. I've had lunch quite a few times with my mom and grandmother. I can't think of anything else to do, frankly."

He studied her with amused eyes. "Don't know what to do with leisure time?"

"It's not something I have a lot of experience with," she replied with a shrug. "Nor interviewing housekeeper applicants either, but I figure it can't be all that hard to talk to a few and set up appointments for you with some of the better ones."

"Did you hire your housekeeper through an agency or on your own?"

"Neither. My mom sent her to me," she admitted with a laugh. "They go to the same church, and my mom knew Carole was looking for someone to fill an opening in her client list. Carole has ten or twelve clients she cleans for, usually on a weekly or every-two-week basis. She likes variety, which is why I said she wouldn't be interested in a full-time position for one client."

He chuckled. "Don't worry, I won't try to steal your housekeeper away."

"I appreciate that," she responded with a smile. "I keep the house fairly neat—mostly because I'm not here enough to make a mess—but I hate doing the heavy cleaning she does twice a month."

Picking up her tea mug again, she said, "I'd be happy to do some interviews for you, Seth. It seems like a helpful, neighborly thing to do."

Her wording made him laugh and relax, as she'd intended. They needed to keep things light and comfortable between them for now. She had agreed to help him because she had the time and he needed the assistance. There was no reason for either of them to read any more into this plan.

He didn't stay much longer. They discussed details of the housekeeper interviews while they finished their tea, and Seth gave her information on how to contact him at work if she needed him. She walked him to the door afterward, stepping out onto the porch with him as they finalized their plans for her to begin interviews on Monday.

"So if you can narrow it down to two or three good applicants at the most—or even to the one you think is best—that would be incredibly helpful," he summed up, juggling his car keys in his hand. "A nonsmoker, willing to work five and a half days a week, and maybe an occasional evening when I have late plans and there's no one else to stay with Alice. Holidays off and two weeks summer vacation. Plenty of time to handle personal business or errands during the day, as long as she's on time picking up Alice from school and available to chauffeur her to activities during the summer. Someone good around the house, a decent cook and mostly someone who can be trusted with Alice."

"Absolutely," she assured him. "I'd never recommend anyone I wouldn't trust implicitly with Alice."

He smiled. "That's why I asked for your help with this. I knew you'd understand my priorities."

She returned the smile and repeated, "Absolutely."

"You're sure you don't mind?"

"Seth." She rested a hand lightly on his arm to emphasize her words. "It's settled. I'll help you. Don't give it another thought."

"Thanks, Meagan. I'll owe you big time for this."

She laughed. "Don't think I won't collect someday."

He shifted his weight, and she realized suddenly how close they stood. Her hand was still on his arm. She started to move it, but he covered it with his own before she could step back.

"You can collect any time," he said, his voice a little lower now, his gaze locked with hers.

"Oh, um…" Her mind seemed suddenly as dim and shadowy as the world beyond the porch lights. "Thanks."

His smile deepened at the corners, and her heart rate sped a little faster. Seth was a nice enough looking guy, anyway, but when he smiled…like this…wow.

Still looking into her eyes, he lowered his head a little more. Very slowly, giving her plenty of time to draw back or turn her cheek, if she wanted. She tilted her face upward, instead.

His lips brushed hers lightly. It was a friendly kiss, neither demanding nor tentative. Yet when it ended, and he drew back to smile at her again, she felt very much as if they'd just stepped over an invisible line between friendly neighbors and something a little more…intimate.

"Good night, Meagan," he murmured and turned away, leaving her hand grasping empty air. She lowered it quickly to her side, stepping into her house and closing the door without waiting to watch him drive away.

Chapter Six

Jacqui Handy was younger than the applicants Meagan had interviewed previously, and that was one of the initial strikes against her. Meagan's preset images of the perfect housekeeper for Seth and Alice was an older woman, much like Nina. Gray haired, sturdy bodied, efficient and congenial—a walking TV housekeeper stereotype, she admitted to herself.

Jacqui was about as far from Meagan's preconception as it was possible for her to be. In her late twenties, she was elfin delicate in build. Her face was dominated by dark eyes and a stubborn-looking, slightly-pointed chin, both features highlighted by short, spiky dark hair. She wore a scoop-neck white knit top with dark jeans and black flats. The garments were obviously inexpensive, but immaculately clean and neatly pressed. Her fingernails were short and unpolished and her hands, while slender and graceful, still looked as though they had known hard work.

"You understand that Mr. Llewellyn is looking for someone who'll stay on for a while?" Meagan emphasized. "His last housekeeper was with him for several years, and would be still if she hadn't been injured."

"I understand that." Jacqui's voice was quiet, but not shy. She met Meagan's gaze steadily, sitting up very straight in her chair in Meagan's living room. "I'm looking for a full-time position. I've moved around quite a bit in my past and I'm ready to stay in one place. I'm good at housekeeping and I'm a good cook. I'll admit I haven't had a lot of experience with children, but you said Mr. Llewellyn's daughter is a teenager? That shouldn't be a problem."

Intrigued, Meagan glanced down at the résumé again. Jacqui hadn't exaggerated when she'd said she'd moved around a lot. According to the jobs she'd listed, she'd worked since she was a teenager, and in at least five different states. She had attached copies of three letters of references from former employers, all highly complimentary of her work ethic. She'd tried everything from retail to food service to hotel staff, but she'd started housekeeping three years ago, when she was only twenty-five. Her last position had been almost a year as a live-in housekeeper for an elderly man who'd finally had to go into a long-term care facility. In the most recent reference letter, the man's daughter had written glowingly about Jacqui's service and dedication to her responsibilities.

"You've certainly made a good impression in your former positions."

Once again, Jacqui answered without looking away. "Not all of them. I gave you all the contact numbers and most of them will say good things about me, but some will say I'm stubborn and insubordinate. I'm pretty easy to get along with for the most part, but I don't like seeing other people mistreated and I won't put up with employers making passes at me or anything like that."

Amused by her tone, Meagan bit the inside of her mouth for a moment before responding. "You wouldn't have to worry about that from Mr. Llewellyn. His daughter and her welfare are paramount to him. He would never step out of line with someone he trusts with her care."

Maybe she hadn't known Seth long, but Meagan was confident she spoke nothing less than the truth. He would never risk hurting or embarrassing his daughter with inappropriate behavior. She wouldn't doubt Jacqui had been subjected to unwelcome attention from former employers, but she was confident that wouldn't happen should Seth decide to hire her. Which didn't mean he wouldn't find Jacqui attractive, she thought with another glance at the pretty young woman sitting across from her. He was a man, after all.

The doorbell chimed suddenly and repeatedly, interrupting the interview. Glancing at her watch, Meagan stood. "That will be Alice now. One of the grandmothers from her school has been giving her a ride home in the afternoons until Seth, er, Mr. Llewellyn hires a replacement housekeeper. She's been spending time with me until her dad gets home from work."

Jacqui nodded. "I'd like to meet her."

"Of course."

It was Wednesday afternoon, and Alice had come over every day that week. Meagan didn't mind. She had offered, after all. She'd even gotten into the habit of having a healthy after-school snack ready. She remembered how hungry she'd always been at the end of a school day.

Carrying a heavy-looking backpack on one shoulder, Alice had already been home and changed out of her school uniform and into a pair of shorts and a T-shirt. Meagan knew the girl wore a bathing suit beneath the shorts. Alice worked on homework at Meagan's kitchen table while she had her snack, but she always wanted a quick swim before she returned home. Meagan teased her about being part fish.

By unspoken agreement, they'd accepted that Waldo wouldn't be a particularly good indoor house guest during these peaceful afternoons. Though she checked on him every afternoon as soon as she got home, Alice left the dog at home, waiting to play with him in the evenings after dinner with her father. She had said repeatedly that she couldn't wait until school let out in June and she could spend whole days with her pet again.

Meagan had reminded Alice several times that she would be back at work next week, but she wasn't sure Alice truly understood how many hours a day Meagan spent at the hospital. She hoped Alice wouldn't be too disappointed when Meagan was no longer available every day for companionship. It would be a good thing if Alice bonded well with the new housekeeper, since they'd be spending so much time together. Someone who could take her to movies or shopping or for other fun summer activities, she thought, glancing thoughtfully behind her to where Jacqui waited.

She tried not to think about how much she would miss Alice. She had enjoyed getting to know the girl during the past three and a half weeks, but it would be hard to sustain their unconventional friendship once Meagan was back at work full time.

She introduced Alice and Jacqui, then discreetly watched them interact. Jacqui was as straightforward with Alice as she had been with Meagan. "I don't have much experience as a nanny, but you look old enough to take care of yourself for the most part."

Alice stood a little taller. "I can take care of myself. But I can't drive yet, so I need someone to take me to things like my friends' parties and dentist appointments and stuff. And I'm going to be on a swim team this summer, so I'll have to go to practice real often. My dad's going to try to be at as many swim meets as he can, but he can't make all the practices."

Jacqui nodded. "I could handle that. I was on a dive team, myself, at one of the schools I attended. I enjoyed it."

"Yeah?" Alice looked intrigued. "I haven't tried the fancy dives yet. I'm a little afraid of the high board. But I can swim laps pretty fast."

"The high board's scary at first," Jacqui agreed. "But you get used to it once you know how to slice into the water."

"You look pretty young."

Jacqui didn't seem to mind the blunt comment. "I'm twenty-eight. Older than I look."

"How come you want to be a housekeeper? Most housekeepers are old, like Nina."

Shrugging, Jacqui replied. "It's a good job. I like keeping things clean and organized and I like to cook. No boss hanging over my shoulder micromanaging my every move. Not a high pressure position. And I usually have some time for myself during the day to read or knit or something while food is cooking or laundry's going. Why wouldn't I like it?"

Alice's face lit up. "You knit?"

"Yes. I make sweaters and scarves and hats. A friend owns a kitschy little boutique in Santa Fe, and she sells my stuff in her shop. And I make some sales over the internet. It's a nice hobby for making some extra spending money."

"Nina was going to teach me how to knit. We only had a couple of lessons before she broke her leg."

"I could teach you, if your dad hires me."

Alice turned eagerly to Meagan. "Can't you hire her, Meagan? I like her."

Meagan held up both hands quickly. "All I'm doing is interviewing and making some recommendations, Alice. Your dad wants to meet the top two or three applicants and decide for himself who to hire. Jacqui knows that."

Jacqui nodded. "I'd want to meet him, too, before I'd take the job, Alice. You know, just to make sure everyone knows what to expect."

Remembering her comment about employers making passes, Meagan suspected Jacqui would want to reassure herself that Seth wouldn't be a problem in that respect. Even though Meagan had promised her that wouldn't be an issue, Jacqui seemed like the type who would want to confirm for herself.

"I'm going to recommend you as one of the applicants for Seth to interview," she said on a sudden impulse. "I'll give him your number so he can set up a time to meet with you this weekend, if that's convenient with you. He wants to make his decision by Sunday, if possible."

"That would be great." Jacqui's dazzling smile made her look so pretty that Meagan had a momentary qualm about her decision. Not that she'd changed her mind about Seth's behavior, but maybe that gray-haired senior citizen she'd envisioned would be a better choice, anyway.

And then she wondered in exasperation why she should care in the least that Seth might find another woman attractive. Or that Alice just might bond with another woman. Nina was the one being replaced, not herself. Her own role in Seth and Alice's life was fleeting, at best, she thought, trying to ignore the hollow feeling that thought left in the pit of her stomach.

Because of an unexpected cancelation, Seth got away from the office a little earlier than usual Thursday. He drove away from the parking lot in a good mood, thinking of the extra time he'd have to spend with his daughter.

The days were growing longer as May wound to a close, and the neighborhood was active on this warm afternoon. The drone of lawnmowers underlay the scents of fresh-cut grass and charcoal grills. His neighbors were taking full advantage of the nice weather in preparation for the rain predicted for the weekend, he thought with a smile. He should get outside and play with Alice and Waldo for a while this afternoon.

Alice and Waldo were already outside, he realized, spotting them in Meagan's front yard as he drove down his street. Meagan stood nearby, watching and applauding while Alice walked Waldo up and down the driveway on his leash. They were all smiling and looked like they were having a great time—even the dog. Alice had worked with Waldo every day since he'd started obedience training, walking him on the leash, firmly repeating commands, rewarding him with praise and pats, as she'd been instructed to do. Her efforts were beginning to pay off.

On an impulse, Seth parked at the curb and climbed out of his car. "Hello, ladies. And Waldo."

Alice whirled with a flash of braces. "Hi, Dad! You're early. Cool. Did you see me walking Waldo? He's doing great."

Seth moved to stand beside Meagan, exchanging smiles of greeting with her. "Let's see it again."

Waldo strained at the leash, trying his best to bound over

to greet Seth with barks and licks. Her feet firmly planted to keep the dog from toppling her over, Alice tugged on the leash to get his attention. "Come on, Waldo. Heel."

It took a couple of repeated commands but he cooperated eventually, dutifully walking at her left side and sitting whenever she stopped walking as he was being trained to do in obedience classes. After she'd walked him up and down the driveway a few times, Alice ordered Waldo to sit, then dropped her end of the leash, repeating the word "stay" as she backed away from him. The dog whined and twitched a little, but stayed where she'd left him until she told him to "break." The moment he heard the word, he bounded from his spot and dashed toward Seth.

Seth caught the dog in midleap, saving his face from being swiped by an eager, wet tongue. "Down, Waldo. Good boy."

Alice caught the trailing leash to keep her pet from running toward the road. "He's doing a lot better, isn't he, Dad?"

"Much better." He glanced again at Meagan. "Maybe I won't have to send him to doggie military school, after all."

"Daddy."

Still looking at Meagan, he asked, "Did you roll your eyes that way when you were her age?"

"Every teenage girl has that mastered," Meagan replied lightly.

"Must be in the genes."

She laughed. "I suppose it is."

"Did Nina leave the hospital today, Dad?"

He turned to Alice and nodded. "She did. I went by to see her on my lunch break, while Lisa was helping her get ready to go. Nina said to tell you she'd send you a computer message as soon as she's settled into her daughter's house."

Alice nodded, her smile gone now. Seth had taken her to say her own goodbyes the night before, and it had been a difficult visit for all of them. Nina had been so much a part of their family.

Meagan spoke brightly. "I have salsa chicken in the oven for dinner. It should be ready in about…" She checked her watch. "…ten minutes. I'd love it if you both could join me."

It wasn't the first time she'd cooked dinner for them that week. Seth had assured her he could manage to feed himself and Alice, but she'd argued that she didn't mind. It gave her something to do with herself during this last week of her sick leave.

Alice's expression brightened, which made Seth even more grateful for Meagan's well-timed invitation. "We'd love to, wouldn't we, Dad?"

"You don't have to twist my arm. We appreciate the offer, Meagan—even though you didn't have to go to all this trouble for us."

She shrugged. "I have to eat, anyway. And this recipe makes too much for one, so I only get to have it myself when I'm cooking for company."

"I'll take Waldo home and then I'll be right back, okay?" Alice said, tugging at her dog's leash again.

"Make sure the gate locks behind you so he doesn't get out," Seth warned automatically.

With another roll of her eyes, Alice muttered, "I will, Dad."

Seth met Meagan's gaze and both of them sputtered a laugh as Alice led her dog away.

Meagan led Seth into the house. She invited him to sit in the living room and relax while she finished in the kitchen, but he chose to give her a hand instead, figuring that was the least he could do. Accepting his offer, she had him set the table while she completed the meal preparation.

Meagan opened the oven door and carefully removed a bubbling casserole dish, filling the kitchen with a savory scent. She carried the dish to the table, setting it on a decorative trivet.

"Wow, that smells good." He hadn't realized how hungry he was until the aroma of her casserole surrounded him.

"It's my mom's recipe. One of my favorite dishes. I figured you and Alice like Mexican food since you were having enchiladas the first time I joined you for dinner."

"We like just about any kind of food," he said with a shrug, then glanced at the table again. "I can tell we're going to enjoy this."

"I hope so." She set a salad bowl filled with chopped tomatoes, red onions and cilantro on the table. "I don't cook often, but I like making something from scratch on occasion."

"I cook on weekends, but usually it's just simple stuff. Spaghetti, burgers, steaks, fish. I make a pretty mean chocolate pie, though. Nina taught me when we learned that Alice was moving in with me. Alice loves chocolate pie."

Pouring iced tea into glasses, Meagan looked over her shoulder at him. "Do you make meringue?"

"Of course. I pile it high—at least four inches."

"I can never make a decent meringue. Mine always weeps."

"Got to make sure your pie filling is hot and that you have a good seal with the meringue around the edges. Nina takes special pride in her meringue and she made me practice until I got pretty close to hers. I'll have to make a pie for you sometime."

Setting the tea glasses on the table, she smiled at him. "I'd like that."

Their gazes met and held for a long moment. Seth found himself indulging in a random fantasy about feeding bites of pie to Meagan—followed by a few lingering, chocolate-flavored kisses. He hadn't had a chance to kiss her since they'd parted the night after the charity gala, though he'd certainly thought of doing so again since. He shifted uncomfortably on his feet when Alice burst into the room, already prattling a mile a minute.

Clearing his throat, he took his seat at the table, trying to rein in his ill-timed, overheated imagination.

Alice was in rare form as they began to eat, chattering nonstop about school, about swim team, about Waldo and about her friends. Meagan was in a good mood, too, making several humorous comments that had them all laughing. His tie and coat abandoned, collar unbuttoned and sleeves rolled back, Seth felt the stress of the workday seep slowly out of him during the leisurely meal.

He decided he could sit there for several hours just watching Alice and Meagan chatting and eating. A passing mention on Meagan's part about returning to work on Monday reminded him how unlikely it was that there would be many more meals like this one once her leave was over and he had a new housekeeper to cook for him and Alice.

"You'll be at work all day Monday, Meagan?" Alice asked, her thoughts seeming to take a similar path to Seth's.

Dabbing at the corners of her mouth with a colorful linen napkin, Meagan nodded. "Yes. I'll be seeing patients in the morning and I have a couple of meetings to attend Monday afternoon. I won't be back at my full schedule until later in the week, but it will feel good to be back at work. I've missed my coworkers and my patients."

"Will you operate on anyone Monday?"

"I don't expect to. I'll be back in the O.R. Tuesday."

"You really cut people open and take stuff out of them?"

Meagan exchanged an amused glance with Seth in response to Alice's slightly appalled expression. "Yes, I do, when it's necessary for their health."

"Have you ever passed out? Because even though I think surgery would be really interesting, I'm afraid I'd pass out if I had to cut someone open and see all the blood and guts and everything."

Seth grimaced around a bite of salsa chicken. "Alice."

Meagan only smiled in understanding. "I've never passed out, but I have to admit the first operations I observed back in medical school were a little difficult. You get used to it, though."

"I haven't decided yet what I'm going to do. Since Mom and Dad are both lawyers, some people assume I'll do that, but I'm not so sure. I think orthodontia is sort of interesting."

Meagan's eyebrows rose in surprise. "Orthodontia?"

Knowing he was about to be in trouble, Seth grinned mischievously. "I think Alice has a crush on her orthodontist. According to the way she described him to her best friend, Jessica, Dr. Samuel is hot."

"Daddy!"

The outraged exclamation—accompanied by a classic eye roll—was exactly what he'd expected in response to his teasing. He laughed unrepentantly.

Meagan leaned a little closer to his red-cheeked daughter, lowering her voice to a conspiratorial just-us-girls tone. "Is he really cute?"

Alice sighed, then frantically fanned her face in illustration. "Totally."

"Maybe I should take you to one of your appointments sometime," Meagan quipped.

Seth felt his smile fade. "And maybe I should start looking for an older and uglier orthodontist for my impressionable daughter."

"Daddy." But Alice giggled this time, sharing a look with Meagan, and Seth tried to ignore the feeling that had come uncomfortably close to unwarranted jealousy at the thought of Meagan checking out Alice's orthodontist.

The conversation wound around eventually to the search for a new housekeeper.

"I talked to the last applicant this morning," Meagan reported. "Theresa Washington. I've added her name to the top three or four I think you should look at more closely. I'll give you the envelope with all the applications and the names of my top suggestions before you leave this evening."

Seth nodded. "I'll call tomorrow and start setting up interviews for this weekend. I can't tell you how much I appreciate your help with this."

Before she could respond, Alice spoke up, a frown on her face now. "I've already told you who you should hire, Dad. Jacqui Handy. She's the one I want."

They'd had this discussion the evening before when Alice hadn't been able to stop talking about the applicant she had met at Meagan's house that afternoon. He'd told her then—numerous times—that while he would keep her opinions in mind, he still intended to interview several people and choose the one he thought would be best for the job. He could see now that she was still determined to convince him to hire Jacqui.

"Meagan thinks she's the best, too, don't you, Meagan?"

Meagan corrected Alice hurriedly. "I've told you, it's up to your father who to hire. I agree that he should meet Jacqui, but there were others I think are equally well suited to the position."

"I will definitely want to interview several." He looked at Alice as he spoke. As important as her opinion was to him, he wasn't leaving the hiring of a housekeeper/nanny in the hands of his thirteen-year-old daughter. "We discussed this last night."

She pouted. "You can talk to them, but you'd be wasting your time. Jacqui's the best one."

"Mrs. Keppler was very nice, too, Alice," Meagan assured her. "I liked her very much."

Alice groaned. "Too old."

"You didn't even meet her."

"You told me about her. You said she has grandkids my age."

"I thought that would be a plus. It means she has experience with teenagers. Maybe you could meet them sometime and make friends with them."

"I have friends at school. I'd rather have someone younger to hang out with at home. Someone who'd take me shopping and wouldn't try to get me to buy ruffly pink dresses."

Catching the not-so-subtle shot aimed directly at him, Seth grimaced a little but kept his attention on Meagan. "Just how young is this candidate Alice likes so much? Alice hasn't directly answered that question when I've asked."

"In her late twenties. But she seems older—you'd have to meet her to quite understand."

Late twenties? Even younger than he'd guessed. Seth studied Meagan skeptically across the table. "I was actually thinking of hiring someone older."

She nodded. "I know. I was hesitant about her age at first, too. But, I think you should give her a chance. She's... interesting."

"Her age doesn't even matter all that much. I liked her," Alice insisted, her tone uncharacteristically stubborn. "And I'm the one who'd have to spend the most time with her, after all."

"And I'm the one who will be paying her," Seth responded firmly. "I'm the one who'd be trusting my daughter and my home to her care. I'll interview her, but if I decide one of the other applicants is more qualified, you'll just have to accept my choice. I'm sure all the top applicants are nice people. I doubt Meagan would recommend someone she thought you wouldn't like."

"Of course not," Meagan confirmed quickly. "The two other women who top my list of recommendations are both very nice. Marilyn Keppler has a great sense of humor and a smile you can't help but respond to. Theresa Washington is a little quiet, but I got the impression that she's very capable and organized, both traits that were mentioned repeatedly in her reference letters."

"But you'll talk to Jacqui, Dad?" Alice repeated, still looking prepared to mutiny. "You'll give her a fair chance?"

"I said I would, and I will," he promised again, hoping this wouldn't be a major problem. Alice had never caused him any real trouble, but she was just becoming a teenager, after all. According to those warnings he'd received from more experienced parents, he was going to have to brace himself for cold shoulders, slammed doors and it's-not-fairs. All things he'd never expected from his sweet-natured daughter, but one never knew what would happen when hormones took over, apparently.

"I have some fresh sliced strawberries and angel food

cake for a light dessert," Meagan said, smoothly directing the conversation away from the potential quarrel. "Who wants some?"

"Sounds good to me." Seth directed a look at Alice, who sighed lightly and nodded, accepting that the argument was over. For now.

They didn't stay long after dessert. Saying she would feed and then play with Waldo, Alice dashed ahead toward home while Seth paused a moment to speak with Meagan at her door. "Thanks for feeding us again. Dinner was delicious."

She smiled up at him. "You're welcome. I enjoyed the company."

"I owe you a few meals now—not to mention all you've done to help me in the housekeeper search." He made a vague motion with the manila envelope filled with applications from all the women she had screened for him.

"It really wasn't that difficult. I just chatted with a few women. The most suitable choices were fairly obvious."

"You keep saying the top three are equal choices in your opinion. You're sure you don't have a personal favorite?"

She gave a little shrug and a wry smile. "I don't want to influence your decision that much," she admitted.

"This Jacqui that Alice likes so much—you said you put her in your top three?"

"I did. I think you'll understand why once you meet her. I'm not saying she's a better choice than the other two—but I do think she's equally qualified."

He smiled. "You sounded more like a lawyer than a doctor just then."

"Heaven forbid."

Chuckling, he tucked the envelope beneath his arm. "I was just thinking—since Alice is going to be at her grandparents' house this weekend…"

Meagan lifted an eyebrow, and he finished hastily, "Maybe I could take you out for a nice dinner Saturday evening?"

She took a moment to think about it—mentally reviewing her calendar? Trying to figure out a way to politely decline?—and then she nodded. "That sounds nice."

He smiled, wondering if there was ever an age when a guy didn't get a little nervous about asking out an attractive woman. "Great. It's the least I can do after all you've done for me."

A little frown appeared between her eyebrows and he spoke quickly again, not wanting her to think he was asking her out only because he felt like he owed her. "I mean, I'll enjoy having dinner with someone, since Alice will be out of town and I...uh."

No. He winced. That wasn't a bit better.

Meagan laughed softly. "You lawyers have such an eloquent way with words."

He smiled ruefully, knowing she'd just gotten him back for the crack he'd made to her. "Touché."

"Good night, Seth. Tell Alice I'll see her tomorrow."

He looked at Meagan's mouth, wanting nothing more at that moment than to kiss her smiling lips. But because he wasn't entirely sure Alice wasn't looking back at them, wondering what was keeping him so long, he restrained himself to a fleeting touch against Meagan's soft cheek. "Good night."

He turned and walked away from her with a reluctance that was starting to feel all too familiar the more time he spent with her. Maybe Saturday night, he wouldn't have to be in such a hurry to leave.

* * *

It was getting a little too easy to be with Seth, Meagan thought sometime late Saturday evening. She'd known the man less than a month. Should it feel so familiar to sit across a dinner table from him? To dance with him afterward at a small, dimly lit, live-music club? Should they have so many little private jokes already? Seemingly random things that made them look at each other and smile each knowing what the other was thinking?

They had shared a few meals and one brief kiss. She had helped him with his daughter and his housekeeper search, he had taken her to a charity dance and out for dinner a couple of times, both with and without his daughter. That was the extent of their...relationship, for want of a better word. She'd spent more one-on-one time with patients.

And yet...

His gaze met hers across the tiny table in the colorfully-lit music bar and he smiled. Her heart tripped.

And yet.

The band launched into a song that was too loud to encourage conversation, but Seth made himself clear enough when he motioned to ask if she wanted to dance again. She thought about it a moment, then held up one finger to indicate that she was up for one more. He grinned, stood, and held out his hand.

She laid her hand in his, their fingers intertwining as they maneuvered their way onto the crowded dance floor. They had chosen a club that didn't skew too young; most of the others surrounding them were in their late twenties through late thirties. Meagan's dark jeans and floaty black-and-red-print top fit in just fine with the crowd, as did Seth's khakis and casual shirt. The band was loud but talented. Meagan enjoyed both the music and the dancing, and the place served an excellent strawberry margarita.

Because he was driving, Seth ordered only a beer and he nursed that slowly during the evening, munching on chips and salsa along with it.

As low-key as the evening was, Meagan couldn't remember the last time she'd enjoyed a date so much.

Seth held her close when they danced, and she suspected that was only partially because there was no room for them to move farther apart. He seemed to be enjoying the evening as much as she was. Already her thoughts were racing ahead to the moment when he would walk her to her door. Alice was gone for the night, so there would be no need for him to rush home. She could ask him in for coffee or... something.

His hand moved against the small of her back and she felt a rush of heat flow from that spot through her veins. His eyes gleamed in the flickering club lights, the green darkened to smoky emerald in the shadows. She couldn't quite read the expression there, but she could make a guess at his thoughts if they were anything like her own.

The club was still rocking when they left a few minutes later, but Meagan was ready to go. As much fun as it had been, her ears had been assaulted enough for one evening. They were ringing a little when she strapped herself into Seth's car, and as a physician she knew that wasn't good for her long-term hearing. But she went to a club maybe twice a year and lived quite sensibly the rest of the time, so she would have no regrets about having had a little fun this evening.

They hadn't talked much about Alice that evening, nor about the search for a housekeeper or any of the other daily responsibilities either of them faced. By unspoken agreement they'd kept their conversations light and diverse, talking of music and books and films, touching on politics and current events, sharing a few tidbits that gave them a little more insight into each other. Conversation for adults enjoying each other's companionship, with no outside responsibilities for just that one evening. She kept her phone nearby in case she was needed and she had no doubt that Seth did the same, but the devices stayed mercifully silent during those few hours.

Seth was the one who brought them back to reality during the drive home. "So, I hired a housekeeper this afternoon."

She hadn't even thought to ask how the interviews had gone that morning, which only showed how captivated she was by Seth himself. "Who did you hire?"

"Got a guess?"

Something about his wry tone made her smile and say, "Jacqui."

"Yeah."

"Alice convinced you?"

"I can't say I wasn't influenced by Alice's opinion. But once I met Jacqui, I saw why you and Alice both thought she'd be good for the job. She has a way of inspiring confidence, doesn't she?"

Meagan laughed softly, remembering Jacqui's direct gaze and self-possessed demeanor. "She does."

"She is young—and at first glance, looks even younger than she is. I hope that doesn't mean she'll get bored quickly and move on, but she said she's looking for a long-term position. She was with her last employer for almost a year, so that's encouraging."

"She certainly had some glowing recommendations."

"She did. I called a couple of them yesterday, after I set up the interview with Jacqui this morning, and everyone I talked with spoke highly of her."

Meagan nodded. "I'm not really surprised. I read the letters she provided."

"She couldn't be more different than Nina."

"Not much."

"Maybe that's a good thing. It would be hard for anyone to stand up to a direct comparison to Nina, as we might have been tempted to do with some of the older women who applied. This way we're really starting fresh."

Meagan studied his profile as he drove, glad he was the one who'd made the final decision, and not her. It had to have been difficult to choose someone with whom to trust his home and his daughter, as he'd pointed out to Alice the other night. "Are you nervous about it?"

He shrugged. "Not really. If it doesn't work out, I'll just blame you."

She blinked a couple of times, then smiled wryly in response to his grave teasing. "Might I remind you who made the final decision? It wasn't me."

"Okay, I'll blame Alice. She threatened to move outside into Waldo's doghouse if I didn't hire Jacqui. I half believed she would."

"She really took to Jacqui." Meagan was aware again of a fleeting ripple of what felt a bit too much like jealousy. Alice had been so attached to her for the past three and a half weeks, but she was aware of the fickleness of youth. And it was just as well, she assured herself. Once she was back at work, the leisurely afternoons by the pool had to end, anyway. It was good that Alice would have another woman to look after her and serve as a role model for her.

Seth chuckled. When Meagan looked at him questioningly, he explained, "Alice could be surprised when Jacqui starts the job. Yes, Jacqui's young and pleasant, but I got the impression she's not going to let Alice get away with much. I told Jacqui I'd expect her to enforce our house rules, and she assured me she would. She said she remembers some of the tricks she pulled as a teenager, so she'll be ready if Alice tries them."

Meagan laughed. Thinking of Jacqui's no-nonsense attitude when it came to inappropriate behavior from employers, she had no doubt Jacqui could handle a teenager, especially one as generally well behaved as Alice.

Seth parked in Meagan's driveway and walked her to the door. The moment of decision, she thought, fingering the keys in her hand.

She glanced at him through her lashes, and he smiled at her. She had been a pushover for that smile from the first night she'd met him. She let out a breath she'd been holding since she'd climbed out of his car.

"Would you like to come in?"

Seth's smile deepened. "Yes. I'd like that very much."

Chapter Seven

Meagan set down her bag and keys and turned to Seth as he closed the front door behind them. "How does decaffeinated green tea sound?"

His hands in his pockets, he studied her face. "Great." He followed her into the kitchen. "Anything I can do to help?"

Very aware of him standing not far away, she drew two mugs from the cabinet, feeling a sense of déjà vu from the last time she'd made tea for him. This routine, too, was becoming a little too familiar considering the short time they had known each other. She wasn't sure why she couldn't just relax and enjoy the time with him, why she couldn't simply appreciate the growing intimacy between them. Yet an uneasy feeling nagged at the back of her mind, some qualm she couldn't quite understand.

"That instant hot water spout is convenient," Seth commented. His voice was even closer than she'd expected. He must have moved closer to examine her hot-water dispenser as she filled the tea pot in which she had placed a diffuser filled with green tea leaves.

She cleared her throat, telling herself she couldn't really feel the heat emanating from Seth's body behind her. He wasn't standing *that* close. It was simply her own over-heated imagination warming her skin.

"It is handy," she agreed, hoping her voice didn't sound as husky to him as it did to her. "I use it all the time."

He reached around her to push the lever, watching as steaming water streamed from the spout before he cut it off again. "Maybe I should think about getting one."

His right arm brushed against her left with his actions. Both wore short sleeves, so that skin touched skin. Accidental contact, she assured herself quickly. Fleeting, at that. Which meant there was no reason at all that every nerve ending in her left arm should be tingling now.

When was the last time the brush of a man's arm had left her tingling? It had been a while, she decided. She'd almost forgotten how nice it felt.

Deciding the tea had steeped long enough, she poured some into a mug and turned to hand it to Seth. He still stood close enough that she barely had to reach out to hand it to him. Their hands met on the mug, and their gazes met and held. Meagan didn't immediately draw away.

After a momentary hesitation, Seth took the mug from her grasp, then set it on the counter without tasting the hot beverage. Seeing the intent in his eyes, she made no move toward her own tea mug which would have taken her out of his reach in a subtle but very clear way. Instead, she leaned slightly toward him.

The one kiss they had shared before had been light, brief, almost platonic. None of those adjectives fit this one. This was the kiss Meagan had been fantasizing about all evening. The kiss she'd more than half expected—and yet had anticipated with an undercurrent of the tension she couldn't explain.

Her hands slid up Seth's chest and around his neck as his arms went around her, nestling her against him. He took his time kissing her. No rush, no pressure for more than a slow exploration of lips and mouths. His hand moved at the small of her back, but only in small, soothing circles, no roaming out of bounds. Seth was clearly leaving it up to her whether this progressed beyond a pleasant kiss in the kitchen.

Maybe it still would before the evening was over...but not yet.

She drew back enough to be able to speak. "Why don't we take our tea into the living room?"

His mouth quirked and his fingers twitched a little against her back, but he merely nodded and moved away, reaching again for his tea.

They sat side by side on the couch, half turned to face each other, gazes meeting frequently over the tops of their tea mugs. She tried to think of something to say but she seemed to have used up all her small talk for one evening. Seth seemed content to drink tea and smile at her.

The silence wasn't painfully awkward. And it wasn't as if there hadn't been a physical awareness between them earlier. But that kiss had definitely ratcheted up the tension a few degrees.

"I've had a great evening," Seth said, as if following the direction of her thoughts. "It was nice, just the two of us. No social obligations to fulfill, no partners or clients or former patients to make small talk with."

"That was pleasant."

"And as much as I enjoy being with my daughter, it was

nice having a grown-ups only night. Not to mention no Waldo."

She laughed. "I've enjoyed the time we've spent with Alice, but I have to agree that a little Waldo goes a long way."

"I warned Jacqui about Waldo. She said she likes dogs, but I assured her she wouldn't be expected to take care of him. Feeding, bathing and cleaning up after her dog were all conditions of the contract Alice signed when she took on a pet."

"You had her sign a contract?"

He chuckled sheepishly. "Well, yeah. The lawyer in me, I guess."

"I think it's a great idea. My parents required us to take care of our own pets, too—at the risk of losing our privileges if we ever dared to neglect an animal—but they never thought to have us sign contracts."

He shrugged. "It was never an issue when I was growing up. My parents let me have pets once I was old enough to take care of them, but they wanted nothing to do with them. I knew if I didn't take care of the pets, no one else would."

Before she could comment, her phone rang. It was the first time either of them had been disturbed by a phone call all evening, so she supposed she could count herself lucky in that regard. Murmuring an apology, she glanced at the phone screen. Calls coming in this late always worried her. Seeing her mother's number, she lifted the phone quickly to her ear. "Mom?"

"I'm sorry to disturb you so late, Meagan. I hope you weren't already in bed."

"No, I'm not in bed." She didn't meet Seth's eyes. "What's wrong?"

"Is it okay if I give your grandmother some ibuprofen?

She says she has a headache and can't sleep. She got into the chocolate earlier and you know how too much chocolate always gives her a headache."

Relieved there was nothing more to the call, Meagan relaxed. "Yes, you can give her an ibuprofen. One should be enough, but if her head still hurts in a couple of hours give her another. If that doesn't help, call me back."

"Your grandmother again?" Seth asked when she disconnected the call a few moments later.

"She has a headache. Mom's afraid to give her anything without checking with me first."

"Always with you? Not your brother or sister?"

"Only when I'm not available." She shrugged. "I'm the oldest and I've been a doctor the longest, so Mom thinks that grants me seniority or something."

"Lucky you."

She shrugged. "I don't mind, really. I try to help her out when I can. I have to admit I felt guilty after my surgery, when she felt like she had to take care of me as well as Meemaw."

"Meemaw?"

She laughed in response to his teasing repetition. "Well, what did you call your grandparents?"

"I hardly remember."

She set her phone aside, hoping it wouldn't ring again.

"You seem to have completely recovered from your surgery," Seth commented. "No offense, but you looked a little peaked that first night I met you."

Remembering that she'd been exhausted just from carrying Waldo across the street, she grimaced good-naturedly. "Gee, thanks."

"Oh, you were still gorgeous. Just peaked," he teased.

Her cheeks warmed a little in response to the compliment. She was hardly gorgeous—but it was nice to hear him say so anyway, even if he was teasing. "Yes, I've completely recovered. I don't think I'll have any trouble returning to work Monday. I'm looking forward to getting back into the O.R."

"To cut people up and take stuff out of them?"

She laughed at his wicked imitation of Alice. "Yeah, something like that."

"Do you mind if I ask what sort of surgery you had? You've never said—not that it's any of my business, of course."

"I don't mind. I had an ovarian torsion. My left ovary became twisted, which cut off the blood supply. Unfortunately, by the time I sought treatment, it was too late to save the ovary. But the surgery went well and I've recovered with no ill effects, so I was fortunate."

He winced. "Sounds like a painful condition."

"It was," she admitted. "Especially since I waited so darned late to see about it."

"I've heard doctors make terrible patients."

"You've heard correctly," she admitted with a short laugh.

"I'm glad you're okay now."

"Thanks. So am I."

"Alice will miss seeing you almost every day."

"I'll miss her, too. I hope she'll still come by some weekend afternoon when I'm home. My pool is always open for her. She knows the combination to the gate lock, but I've made her promise she won't ever swim alone."

"Thanks. That's one of my rules, too. Maybe Jacqui will come with her sometime, if you really don't mind."

"I don't mind at all. It would be nice to know someone's enjoying the pool."

"I told Alice I'll consider putting one in for next summer. Too much going on to even think about it this year."

"Um—" He'd shifted his weight as he spoke, bringing him a little closer to her. She found it suddenly more difficult to follow the conversation. Who could think about pools when Seth was sitting close enough that his thigh was only an inch or so from her own?

He must have seen something in her expression. He reached out to take her hand in his, lacing their fingers together. Scooting a little closer, he laid an arm along the back of the couch, lowering his face to hers. She rested a hand on his chest, feeling his heart beating beneath her palm. Steady—but maybe just a little accelerated? She'd hate to think she was the only one whose pulse was suddenly racing.

His mouth covered hers, slowly at first and then with more urgency. Even their kisses were becoming more familiar, she thought—the taste of his mouth, the feel of his arms around her, the spicy scent of his aftershave. She felt as though she had known him so much longer than three and a half weeks. And yet she was aware that there was so much about him still to learn.

One kiss led to another. One exploratory caress to the next. Buttons were loosened, heated skin revealed and kissed. Seth's partially-bared chest was broad and smooth, only sparsely matted with brown curls. She spread her hand against him, feeling nice, firm pecs and abs beneath her palm. Though not bodybuilder ripped, the man definitely worked out.

She lay back against the arm of the couch with Seth draped half over her. The hem of her loose top was raised and his hand moved beneath it, carefully avoiding her healing scar, though he dropped a teasing kiss beside it to "make it all better" which made her laugh softly. He toyed with the lacy edge of her bra, then slid his fingers beneath to tease her into hard, aching peaks. Their legs were entangled, and she had no doubt that his body was ready to take these embraces to the ultimate conclusion.

She knew the feeling all too well, she thought, shifting restlessly against him. His lips moved against her throat and she turned her head to give him better access to the tender skin beneath her ear. Her hazy gaze fell on the phone she'd tossed onto the coffee table after her mother's call.

Her hands stilled on Seth's shoulders.

Sensing her change of mood, he lifted his head to study her warm face. "Meagan?"

She sighed regretfully. These past three and a half weeks had been idyllic—which was exactly the reason she hesitated now. She understood now why it had made her vaguely uncomfortable to feel that she was getting to know Seth so well. The problem with that was that she wasn't at all certain the reverse was true.

She had seen Seth in his usual routines. Working every day, dining and playing with his daughter afterward. Networking at a professional social event. Dealing with a family crisis when Nina had fallen. Sometimes rushed or weary but always, apparently, himself.

Seth couldn't say the same about her. The closest he'd come to seeing her at work was when she'd administered basic first aid to Nina. The only time he'd seen her called away was when her mother had called for her to go check on her grandmother, and that had not called her away from anything in particular. She had been at home almost every day since he'd met her, available to take his daughter shopping or to watch her after school, to interview housekeeper applicants and to prepare dinners for the three of them.

This wasn't her life. This was so far from her life that she hardly recognized herself during the past month. So how could Seth know her?

Though he couldn't possibly have followed her thoughts,

Seth could see from her expression that their evening was coming to an end. She watched the resigned realization cross his face before he drew back, straightening her blouse with the movement. He gave her a hand to help her sit beside him.

She wasn't embarrassed, she thought as she watched him shove a hand through his tousled hair and tug at his partially unbuttoned shirt. Nor did she regret anything that had transpired between them that evening. She liked this man very much and would like to think their developing friendship wouldn't end when she returned to her career. But still it seemed best to proceed a bit more cautiously at this point, considering how many big changes were looming.

Seth drew a long, deep breath, as if steadying his pulse and his thoughts. "I guess it's getting late."

She smoothed her hair with a hand still prone to tremble a bit. "It is."

"I won't be around much tomorrow. I'm going to clear away some paperwork in my office in the morning, and I'll be on the road four hours going after Alice and bringing her home."

She nodded. "I'm spending most of tomorrow with my family, since it's the last day of my leave. I've talked Mom into letting me sit with Meemaw while Mom goes to church and out to lunch with some of her friends from there. I'll probably stay for dinner, and my brother and sister are going to try to drop by for a while."

"Nice that you can spend time with them." He rose as he spoke, tugging at the hem of his shirt but not bothering to refasten the top buttons. He looked quite dashing with his sleeves rolled back and his chest half bared. Meagan was briefly tempted to drag him back down to the couch, but she resisted. She'd had good reason to call a halt, she reminded herself.

She walked him to the door. "So, I'll see you around?"

He dropped a hand on her shoulder, looking down at her with a quizzical little smile. "You will most definitely see me around. I'll call you tomorrow evening."

She nodded. "That would be nice."

He bent his head to kiss her good night, his lips lingering softly against hers before he moved away. "Good night, Meagan."

"Good night."

Closing the door behind him, she rested her cheek against the cool wood for a moment, her knees pleasantly wobbly, her skin deliciously hypersensitive. She suspected she would spend the next few restless hours wondering if she'd been an idiot to send Seth away.

Seth's house was dark and quiet when he let himself into the kitchen. He frowned as he tossed his keys on the counter, the resulting clatter seeming to echo through the empty rooms. He'd gotten so accustomed to having Alice living with him full time that he hardly knew what to do with himself when he was here alone.

Waldo barked a couple of times on the other side of the kitchen door, probably having heard Seth moving around inside. Though he'd fed the dog and given him fresh water before leaving for the evening, he opened the door to check on him anyway, using his body to block Waldo from dashing in. A brick patio lay off the kitchen and he sat for a few minutes in one of the patio chairs, rubbing the dog's head and gazing up at the stars. An airplane passed far overhead, lights blinking against the inky sky. In just three short weeks, Alice would be on a plane headed off for a month with her mother.

"We're both going to miss her then, aren't we, pal?" he said aloud to the dog, who licked Seth's fingers and crowded closer.

He supposed he and Jacqui would have to share responsibility for the mutt during that month. He hoped Jacqui had been telling the truth when she said she liked dogs and wouldn't mind helping with Waldo when Alice was away. He hoped *everything* Jacqui had said was truc, he added with a wry twist to his mouth. He still wondered if he'd let himself be overly influenced by Alice's wishes when he'd rather impulsively offered Jacqui the job. But he had to admit Jacqui had certainly inspired confidence.

He chuckled quietly when he remembered the way she had made it very clear that there would be no "funny business" between her and an employer. He had assured her gravely that she need have no concerns in that respect. He hadn't added that while he thought she was attractive, in a gamine sort of way, she wasn't really his type.

His thoughts drifted across the street, to the woman who was very much his type, apparently, since he could not seem to stop obsessing about her.

What had made her call such an abrupt halt to their kisses this evening? He had no doubt that she'd been enjoying their embraces as much as he was, and she'd certainly been an eager participant. But then he'd sensed a sudden change in her mood. She hadn't had to say anything, not even to push lightly against him—he'd simply known it was over.

He sighed, both sorry and somewhat relieved the evening had ended when it had. His disappointed body still ached with needs he hadn't satisfied in quite a while. Yet he reminded himself that he needed to be careful about getting involved in a relationship that could turn out to be a disaster on several levels. He had to think first of Alice.

Had Meagan thought of Alice at just that crucial moment? Or had some other reservation caused her to draw away? Whatever the reason, it probably was best that he'd be spending tonight in his own otherwise empty bed.

Not that he was sleepy yet. Absently tugging at one of Waldo's droopy ears, he felt the adrenaline still pumping through his veins, though his pulse was gradually returning to normal as he relaxed with the blissful dog. It had been a long time since he'd indulged in a "make-out session" on a couch. And damn, it had been fun. He suspected he'd have to pay for the pleasure with a long, restless night ahead— but all in all, he decided it had been worth the price.

Meagan sat in her mother's living room, rocking and reading—or trying to read. The house was peaceful. Her grandmother was napping in her bedroom, and her mother hadn't yet returned home from her outing with her church friends. The book was a good one, with interesting characters and an intriguing mystery but Meagan's attention kept wandering.

As hard as she tried to think about anything but Seth, she wasn't having a great deal of success.

Noise from the kitchen made her close the book, thinking her mother was home a little early. She shook her head in exasperation, hoping her mom hadn't called the outing short because she felt guilty about being away from home for a few hours. Meagan had assured her she would be fine here with Meemaw for several hours, and that her mom should take advantage of the chance to get out. It wasn't often Meagan was free to donate time during the day, even when her mom would allow her to do so.

Prepared to fuss, she sank bank into the chair when her sister dragged into the room. Madison gave her a little wave of greeting, then walked to the couch and made a production of falling face down upon it.

Meagan chuckled. "Rough day?"

Without lifting her head from an embroidered throw pillow, Madison groaned. "Thirty-hour call. Six admissions. One little jerk medical student with a chip on his shoulder."

"Been home yet?"

"No. Wanted to see you and Mom." Madison's voice was muffled and drowsy. Two minutes later, her even breathing told Meagan her sister was asleep.

"Nice to see you, too," Meagan murmured, settling back into the rocker with her book.

Twenty minutes later, Meagan's reading was disturbed again.

"Got your mind on someone...er, something else?"

Lowering the book, Meagan frowned at her sister who had flopped over on the couch and was now watching her with a grin. "What?"

"You've read that same page about three times now, and I bet you still couldn't tell me what it says. Obviously, your attention is wandering."

Meagan closed the book and set it aside. "I guess it is. Just not in the mood to read today."

"So? What *are* you in the mood for today?"

"What are you talking about, Maddie?"

Sitting up, Madison fluffed her work-and-nap-flattened blond hair, looking oddly refreshed from the very short nap. "I heard you had a date with Alice's cute dad last night."

Meagan frowned. She had not mentioned to anyone that she was going out with Seth last night. "How did you find out about that?"

"Julie Castor said she saw you at Joaquina's last night dancing with an attractive man. She said you looked like you were having a very good time, if you know what I mean."

Meagan had not caught even a glimpse of her sister's friend last night, which only served to illustrate just how preoccupied she had been with Seth. Of course, the club had been crowded, she added quickly in her own defense. It was no surprise she hadn't seen every other patron in the room.

"What made you think I was with Alice's dad?" she asked rather lamely. "I do know other men, you know."

"Uh-huh." Madison looked at her.

Meagan sighed. "It was Seth."

"And you're still thinking of him today."

"Maybe."

"Getting serious, sis?"

"I've only known him a little more than three weeks."

"Dad and Mom said it took them only as long as a Klingon saber dance to know they'd found the one."

"Well, I need a little more time than that," Meagan replied dryly. "I'm not actually looking for 'the one.'"

"Everyone's looking for 'the one,' Meg. We just hope we'll know him when we see him—or her, in the guy's case."

"Or that we'll have time to do anything about it when we find him?"

Madison smiled wearily. "There is that. Why did we go to medical school again?"

Before Meagan could answer, she heard her grandmother's quivery voice coming from the back of the house. "LaDonna?"

Madison started to rise. "Want me to check on her?"

"No, just rest. I'll go."

It turned out her grandmother just wanted to know if it was time to take her meds. "You've got another hour,

Meemaw," Meagan assured her. "Mom will be home by then to give them to you."

Her grandmother pulled her sheet to her frail chin. "Okay, then. Maybe I'll sleep a little longer."

"All right." Meagan brushed a kiss against her grandmother's cool, paper-thin skin. "Call me when you want to get up and I'll come help you."

Her grandmother's eyes were already closed. "Thank you, honey."

Meagan half expected to find her sister sleeping again in the living room, but Madison was in the kitchen, making a pot of coffee.

"Shouldn't you go home and get some sleep?"

Madison shrugged. "I will after I've seen Mom. That nap helped."

"Twenty minutes?"

Chuckling, Madison drew cups out of a cabinet. "You know how it goes. We sleep when we can."

"Did you manage to get any sleep last night?"

"An hour. Maybe two."

Meagan leaned against the fridge, studying her sister's always pretty, but pale face. "You aren't dating anyone now, are you?"

Madison's laugh was incredulous. "Like I'd have time to date. But you'd know if I were seeing someone important. Mom would tell you."

"Or your friend Julie would," Meagan murmured wryly.

Madison laughed again. "Julie does have a way of finding out all the latest gossip. She had all kinds of news when she called me this morning. Even a juicy tidbit about one of your partners."

Meagan tried to resist. On principle, she disapproved of gossip and made a habit of not spreading it. As a physician, privacy laws and discretion had been drilled into her from the first day of medical school. But like any workplace, hospitals were rife with coworker gossip and it was hard to resist sampling the occasional morsel. "Um…one of my partners?" she asked casually.

Her expression a little too knowing, Madison nodded. "Stephen Easton. He and Danielle broke up last week."

Meagan almost felt her jaw drop. "They broke up? Seriously?"

"Yeah. Julie said he moved out of the loft Friday."

A year behind her in medical school, Stephen had been engaged to Danielle Carpenter for almost as long as Meagan had known him. Both busy surgeons on a fast track to local prominence, Stephen and Danielle had appeared to be the ideal couple. They both understood the demands of their jobs, they both came from privileged backgrounds, they seemed to have similar goals and ambitions. "The wedding was going to be in August, wasn't it?"

"That's what Julie said. But it's off. Rumor has it that Danielle is taking a position in another state."

Meagan was somewhat surprised she hadn't already heard this news—but then again, if it had only happened on Friday maybe it wasn't so surprising. She hadn't talked to anyone from work yesterday. It was odd, though, that Julie, a nutritionist in the hospital, had heard the scuttlebutt before one of Stephen's partners.

She sighed. So many of her fellow surgeons were single, divorced or in bad relationships. She supposed that was true of many professions—and of course she knew a few happily married surgeons—but it had to be difficult to combine that all-encompassing career with the demands of a long-term commitment.

"If even Stephen and Danielle couldn't make it work, you have to wonder if anyone could," she murmured, thinking aloud.

Her sister shrugged. "I always wondered if a couple who's engaged for four or five years really wants to get married in the first place."

"Still…"

"It's no harder for doctors to sustain a relationship than it is for anyone else," Madison declared firmly. "I've never heard anybody say it's easy, it just takes a lot of work and a determination to beat the odds."

Meagan lifted an eyebrow. "You make it all sound pretty grim."

"There's nothing grim about making a marriage work."

Their mother's voice made both sisters turn in surprise. Meagan hadn't heard her come in and neither had Madison, apparently. Meagan didn't know how long she'd been standing in the doorway leading from the kitchen into the hall, but she'd been there long enough to have heard at least part of their conversation.

"Yes, marriages take work and determination," their mother continued, "but that's true of anything that matters to you. A career, a hobby, a home. You put in the effort because of the joy you get back in return. And my marriage to your father brought me a great deal of joy—even if it wasn't always easy being married to a man whose brilliant and eccentric mind often wandered to other planets."

For just a moment the ghost of the late Timothy Baker seemed to hover in the kitchen, leaving both humor and sadness behind when he drifted away again. Meagan thought she would always remember her wonderfully idiosyncratic father with just that mix of emotions.

"How was your morning out, Mom?"

Accepting a glass of iced tea from Madison, their mother patted Meagan's arm. "It was lovely. Thank you again for sitting with your grandmother. Did you have any problems?"

"No. She had an early lunch of soup and crackers and a small slice of cheesecake, and then she wanted to take her nap."

Madison spoke teasingly to lighten their mom's suddenly grave expression. "Okay, Mom. Tell us all about church and lunch today. I know you've come home with lots of juicy gossip and you know how I love a good gossip session. Meagan never dishes about anyone—including herself," she added pointedly.

Meagan suspected Madison was a little put out that she hadn't heard any more details about last night's date. But while they occasionally talked about their romantic adventures—what few there had been for either of them in the past busy years—she wasn't quite ready to talk about Seth.

Which was only another reason for Meagan to worry that this thing with Seth—whatever it was—was more significant than she wanted to admit to her sister. Maybe even to herself.

Chapter Eight

"You look so well rested! That time off was good for you."

It was at least the fifth time that day Meagan had heard those words, making her wonder just how tired she had looked prior to her emergency surgery. She smiled briefly at the speaker, one of the partners in the surgical practice, as they gathered in a conference room for the first of the two Monday afternoon meetings she was scheduled to attend. "Thanks, Lee. I'm feeling great. Glad to be back at work."

"How are you doing? Holding up okay?"

"Of course. Hitting on all cylinders." She wouldn't have admitted otherwise, of course. She had her pride, after all. And Lee was one of those guys who was inclined to think men were slightly better suited to surgery than women, unless it was gynecological surgery.

"Glad to hear it. Let me know if you need anything, you hear?"

"Absolutely. Thanks."

She wouldn't be asking for help, of course. She really was getting along fine. Maybe a little more tired than she normally would be at this point in the day, but she could ignore that. She suspected she would sleep well that night, tired and satisfied that she'd accomplished something worthwhile again.

It was nice to be back among her colleagues. Her partners, her secretary, the nurses and techs. The weary residents and nervous medical students. The bustling hospital staff. It was good to see patients, to offer advice and reassurance, hope where possible and comfort when hope was slim. Her fingers were already itching to hold a scalpel again, to scrub up for battle in the operating room.

She'd known when she selected to go into surgery as opposed to some other specialty that her hours would be long, almost never less than fifty hours a week and usually a bit more. But she still believed she'd made the right choice. She loved her work, and couldn't imagine doing anything else. It felt so good to be back.

She ran into Stephen Easton a couple of times during the day. Though they were more acquaintances than true friends, he welcomed her back warmly and told her he was glad she had recovered so well. She thanked him politely without mentioning the gossip about him she'd now heard from several sources. It seemed that all their associates were as shocked and surprised as Meagan had been about Stephen's split with Danielle.

She had intended to be back home early that evening but one thing led to another, one meeting to the next. She had dinner with two of her partners, then spent a couple hours in her office catching up on files and notes and making a loose schedule for the rest of the week. Beginning at six-thirty the next morning, she had patients to see, surgeries to perform, residents to teach…in other words, her work life was resuming right where it had left off.

So why did she feel as though something had changed?

Dark was settling over her street when she drove toward her house that evening. Lights burned in the windows of her neighbors' homes. Glancing toward Seth's house as she braked for her driveway, she saw the lights on there, too. She wondered how Jacqui's first day on the job had worked out. Had she been on time to pick up Alice at school, and had they bonded over snacks afterward? Had Jacqui made a good dinner for Seth and Alice?

She pictured father and daughter chatting about their day over the shared meal. What were they doing now? Watching a television program together, perhaps? Or was Alice bent over homework while Seth worked on a brief or a report or whatever attorneys did at home after hours? Maybe they were outside playing with Waldo or sitting in the kitchen indulging in a sweet before Alice's bedtime.

Her own house was dark when she walked into the kitchen. Very quiet. She flipped on the overhead lights, reminding herself to reset timers so there would be a few lights burning when she returned home tomorrow night. She didn't mind living alone, she assured herself, but she'd never liked coming home to a completely dark and empty house.

Pushing aside a mental image of a father and daughter laughing together over cookies or ice cream, she opened the fridge and drew out a small, single-serve container of fat-free yogurt. Maybe the strange feeling of hollowness inside her signaled nothing more than hunger. She couldn't imagine what else it could be, considering how satisfied she was with the life she had chosen.

* * *

Seth called Wednesday evening. It was the first time she'd heard from him since Sunday, when he'd called for a few minutes to let her know Alice was home safely from her grandparents and to wish her luck with her first day back at work.

It was past nine, and she'd been home only twenty minutes or so. She was tired, but in a good way, feeling as though she'd accomplished a great deal that day.

"How's it going?" Seth asked after they'd exchanged greetings. "Back in the swing of things yet?"

"Definitely." She kicked off her shoes and tucked her feet beneath her on the couch. Hearing his voice in her ear reminded her of the last time she'd been with him on this very couch, which made her heart trip a bit. She tried to concentrate on the conversation. "Three surgeries today, all very successful, in addition to rounds, patient visits, a couple of consults, and a quick dinner with my brother in the hospital cafeteria."

"Sounds like a busy day."

"No more than usual."

"I waited until I saw your lights on before calling. Do you usually get home so late?"

"Sometimes earlier, sometimes later. Just depends on my schedule."

"What time do you leave in the mornings?"

"I'm usually at the hospital by six-thirty."

"Long days."

"I work fifty, sometimes sixty hours a week. The surgeon's life," she said. Though she kept her tone light, she was being candid. Seth should know exactly what her schedule was like.

If he was dismayed, he kept it out of his voice. "I understand. I probably put in that many hours, myself, though

I have the luxury of doing some of my work while I'm at home with Alice."

"I do some paperwork at home, but it would be hard to operate in my living room."

He chuckled. "I guess it would be."

Okay, something was coming through in his tone, she decided. His laugh had sounded just a little stilted, his humor a bit forced. Had her hours taken him aback that much, or was she simply imagining those things?

"How are things going over there?" she asked by way of distraction. "How's Alice?"

"She's doing well. Next week's her last week of school, so she's started studying for final exams."

"And Jacqui? How's she doing?"

"So far, so good. She's a cleaning demon, and a very good cook, though different than Nina. Nina cooked a lot of southwestern dishes, Jacqui's cooking has more of a Mediterranean flavor. Really good, though."

"That's great. She and Alice are still getting along well?"

"So far. They're starting knitting lessons as soon as school is out. Apparently, Jacqui is quite the professional knitter."

"She mentioned that when I interviewed her."

"She's a real stickler for schedules, too. She and Alice made out a schedule together for the next two weeks. Snack time, study time, piano practice time, Waldo time. She said they'll make up a new schedule for summer days after school's out."

"How does Alice feel about that?"

"She's not complaining, but the novelty hasn't worn off yet. We'll just have to see how it all works out."

"Tell her I said hello, will you? Both of them, actually."

"I will. So, I'll, um—I'll talk to you later, then."

"It's always nice to hear from you," she assured him, in case there was any doubt.

She couldn't read his tone when he said, "Good night, Meagan. Get some rest."

"I will. You, t—"

But Seth had already hung up.

As she set her phone aside, she felt as though he'd disconnected in more ways than just a phone call. She had noted that he'd made no attempt to arrange another outing with her.

She pushed a hand through her hair. Suddenly she felt much more weary than she had before she'd spoken with Seth.

"I wish we could see Meagan again. Why can't we ask her over for dinner tonight or something?"

Alice's tone made Seth grimace. He recognized that one. She was gearing up for a quarrel, mentally prepared to counter anything he might say.

He had barely gotten in the door Friday evening after work, having walked into the kitchen only a few minutes earlier. He'd thought Alice would be pleased that he'd gotten away from the office a little early, especially since he'd had to work a couple hours late the night before, but her thoughts were on the neighbor she hadn't seen for a week.

He glanced at Jacqui, who was grating parmesan cheese over a pasta, artichoke and caper dish. The scents emanating from the oven were mouthwatering, making him remember he'd had time only for a half a sandwich at lunch. But before he could wash up for dinner, he supposed he had to deal with Alice's mood.

"We can't ask Meagan to dinner because she isn't even home," he said. "I just passed her house."

It wasn't even six-thirty yet; Meagan could be another two hours or so getting home, from what he'd observed so far that week. Not that he'd been watching her house or anything. He'd simply been trying to get an idea of her schedule.

What he had seen had not been encouraging. Nor was the disappointment on Alice's face now.

"Maybe you could call her and see if she's going to be home soon?" she asked hopefully. "I bet she's hungry. She'll probably be too tired to cook for herself tonight. And she hasn't even had a chance to taste Jacqui's cooking yet. I know she'll like it."

"Thank you, Alice," Jacqui murmured, wiping down the countertops without looking around.

Seth shook his head. "I'm not calling her before she gets home. For all we know, she could be operating on someone. Or in an important meeting. I'm not interrupting her."

"But—"

"Alice." He leveled a look at her, the one that told her the conversation was over.

Fortunately, that look still worked on her. She sighed, bit her lip, and shrugged. "All right. Fine. I'll go wash up."

"Good idea."

Alone in the kitchen with Jacqui, he shook his head. "She's a good kid, on the whole, but when she gets an idea in her head she's like a dog with a bone. She's not letting go."

"I noticed." Wringing out her cloth, Jacqui draped it over the back of the sink to dry. "She wanted me to call Dr. Baker earlier and extend an invitation for dinner. I told her that doctors—surgeons—are very important people and can't be disturbed when they're at work, but I'm not sure she understands."

"I'll talk to her again later. She shouldn't be trying to wheedle you into doing things for her."

"I can handle it."

"I'm sure you can."

Jacqui went into the laundry room to collect the oversized knitting bag she brought with her every day. Her car keys dangled from her hand. "You need anything else before I head out?"

"No, we're good here. You're always welcome to join us for dinner, you know." He had made it clear from the beginning that she would be treated more as family than help. While she seemed to appreciate the distinction, she had yet to join them for a meal.

She shook her head. "Thanks, but I have plans."

"Then don't let me keep you."

Funny little thing, he thought after she left. Efficient and self-possessed at one moment, oddly shy at the next. She'd fit into the routine easily enough, though the dynamics were different with her than they had been with Nina. Nina had been motherly, nurturing, sometimes a little meddlesome. Jacqui was more behind-the-scenes, running the household quietly and smoothly, polite but not too familiar. He wouldn't be at all surprised to learn that she'd studied and imitated the behavior of TV butlers.

It was strange how he knew so much about her work history, yet not a lot about her personally. He guessed that wasn't important as long as she did her job well. And he'd only known her a week. She'd probably open up more with time.

"I guess I'm ready to eat," Alice said, rejoining him. "I just looked out the window and I don't think Meagan's home yet," she added.

"I just told you she wasn't."

"But she might have come home since."

"Let's just enjoy our dinner together, okay? Since when do we need anyone else to keep us entertained?"

"I like having dinner with you, Dad," she assured him earnestly, looking suddenly concerned that she might have hurt his feelings. "It's not like we need anyone else. I just miss Meagan, is all."

He tugged fondly at one of her curls, smiling down at her with a cheerfulness he didn't quite feel. This, he told himself, was why he'd been concerned with getting involved with another woman whose career was all-consuming. He hated seeing Alice disappointed.

"Let's eat," he said. "After dinner we'll go out and play with Waldo for a while, if you want, and then maybe watch some TV or play a game or something. Since we've both got a free evening."

Her face brightened. "That sounds like a great evening. I'll pour our drinks. You want iced tea?"

"Of course." He was relieved he'd been able to put a smile back on her face.

He hadn't wanted to admit to her that he missed Meagan, too.

It was a busy weekend for Meagan, as her weekends usually were. She was on call Saturday, and she spent most of the day in the O.R. She had a few emergency lap appy and lap coli surgeries—the shortened reference to laparoscopic appendectomies and cholecystectomies, or removal of the gallbladder—and one splenectomy from a battered young man whose mountain bike had proved no contest to the steep ascent he had attempted.

Even without complications, she found those almost-daily procedures challenging and interesting, but they were only a portion of the operations she performed in her general surgery practice. More complicated procedures could take eight hours or more to perform, on her feet the entire time in a busy operating room, working in a narrow sterile field, surrounded by staff who were there strictly to assist her in providing care to the patient. Time passed quickly when she was focused on her work. Her days never seemed to hold as many hours as she needed to get everything accomplished.

She stayed too busy to spare much thought for Alice and Seth that day. She only wondered about them every hour or so. Only glanced at her phone four or five times to see if she'd missed a call from either of them. Only asked herself a half dozen or so times if the kisses she'd shared with Seth on her couch had been the last time she would ever be that close to him.

So what if his image was the last picture in her mind before she fell into an exhausted sleep that night? So what if he was still in her thoughts when she first awoke the next morning? So maybe she was still a little infatuated with him, but she imagined those feelings would fade with time, just like the scar from the surgery that had indirectly led to her meeting him.

She spent Sunday morning with her mother and grandmother, who was struggling with another illness, a urinary tract infection this time. Though her grandmother resisted, Meagan finally insisted she be taken to the hospital through the emergency department that afternoon. Meagan wasn't at all comfortable with her grandmother's vital signs. She wasn't Meemaw's primary care physician, she insisted. Her grandmother needed hospital care under the supervision of her very capable gerontologist.

Back at the hospital, she checked on a few of her patients while her grandmother was being admitted and evaluated. LaDonna wouldn't leave her mother's side, and Meagan figured she would stay the night in her mother's room.

Meagan still worried almost as much about her mother as she did her grandmother.

She stopped by the coffee shop for a take-out cappuccino for her mom and straight coffee for herself. She knew her mom had a weakness for vanilla cappuccinos and she could probably use the little boost. An insulated cup in each hand, she entered the elevator, only to find her sister already in the car.

"Going up to Meemaw's room?" Madison asked, reaching out to relieve Meagan of the cappuccino.

"Thanks. Yes, I thought Mom could use some liquid energy. Did she call you?"

"Yes. I was at a baby shower for one of the other residents. You know how I hate baby showers, so I said I needed to rush right over."

Meagan smiled wryly. "I was going to call you once we got the lab reports back. I guess Mom called Mitch, too."

"She said she was going to. Not sure what Mitch was doing today, but he'll probably stop by when he can."

"He will, unless he wants to risk one of Mom's disappointed looks."

Madison faked a shudder. "Anything but that."

The car stopped and the only other occupant, a man holding a spray of pink roses, got off. A few people waited on the other side of the sliding doors, but they must have wanted to go down because no one else entered this car. The doors slid shut again.

"How is Meemaw, really?" Madison asked when the car began to rise again.

Meagan shrugged. "Just a UTI, I think, but in her condition…"

"I've been thinking. Maybe it's time to start talking about a hospice referral. More for Mom's sake than Meemaw's, really."

The focus of hospice care was to provide comfort and support for dying patients and their families. Hospice was usually called in when a person was diagnosed as terminal, with six months or less remaining to live. Their grandmother's physician had not yet made that call, but Mcagan suspected he would agree if Meagan and Madison consulted him. She thought six months was rather generous as a prognosis.

"It's going to be tough for Mom to concede the end is getting that close," Madison murmured as the elevator bumped to a stop again. "I've been trying to prepare her, but she keeps thinking one of the treatments will give Meemaw a few more good years."

They fell into step toward their grandmother's room, both nodding greetings to hospital staff they knew and worked with on a daily basis.

"I've hinted, too," Meagan said, "and I think Mitch came right out and told her last weekend, after the respiratory incident, that Meemaw doesn't have much longer. All that seemed to do was make her even more determined to fight for more time. She's been cooking like crazy all week, making Meemaw's favorite foods, coaxing her to eat and spend more time out of the bed. Meemaw's been cooperating as best she could, but you and I both know it's a losing battle."

Madison sighed and nodded sadly.

They found their mom standing in the hallway outside the room. "The nurses asked me to step out for a few minutes while they do someone in there," she explained, looking disturbingly wan. "They said they'd let me know when we can come back in."

"I brought you a cappuccino, Mom. One of the vanilla ones you like." Meagan nodded toward her sister, who pressed the disposable cup she'd carried into their mother's hands.

"Thank you, Meagan. That was very thoughtful of you."

"You're welcome. There's a sitting area at the end of this hallway with some recliners and couches and tables. Let's go wait down there and drink our coffee."

Her mother frowned. "The nurses won't know where to find us."

"I'll go in and check on things," Madison volunteered, moving toward the closed door of the room. "You two go on down and rest a minute."

Reassured, their mother allowed herself to be persuaded to sit for a few minutes with her beverage. Meagan and Madison exchanged looks of concern as Meagan led their mother toward the small sitting area, which was, fortunately, unoccupied at the moment.

Madison rejoined them a few minutes later. "They have her settled comfortably," she reported, motioning her mother to remain seated when she started to rise. "Finish your coffee, Mom, Meemaw's sleeping. She wouldn't even know you were in the room. And don't worry, she'll be fine for a few minutes alone. If she needed constant watching, she'd be in ICU."

Only somewhat reassured, their mom settled back into the chair, though Meagan thought she looked prepared to leap to her feet at a moment's notice.

Madison looked at Meagan with raised eyebrows. Guessing her sister was asking silently if Meagan had talked to her mother about their grandmother's prognosis, Meagan shook her head. She figured they could wait to have that talk after the most recent lab results came back, and after they'd talked to their grandmother's physician.

Getting the message, Madison nodded and spoke

brightly to lighten the heavy mood among them. "How's it going with you and Seth?" she asked Meagan.

Meagan answered vaguely, "I haven't seen him this week. I've been busy back at work, and I'm sure he and Alice have been busy, as well."

"You've talked to him, though, haven't you?"

"Not in the last few days. Like I said, I've been busy."

And Seth had made no effort to contact her, she thought, biting the inside of her lip.

Madison was the one wearing a frown now. "Surely you can make time for a phone call. Or to have dinner with the guy. You're not going to run this one off with inattentiveness like you did Gary, are you?"

Gary was a man Meagan had dated a few times more than two years ago, back when she was still a busy resident. She had liked him, but not enough to completely rearrange her schedules for him. And because he was a man who needed someone to be available pretty much all the time for him, he'd rather quickly acknowledged that perhaps a surgeon wasn't the best choice of companion for him. Meagan had hardly given him a thought since, proving that her feelings for him had been fleeting and rather shallow. Madison, on the other hand, had been disappointed by the breakup—probably because she was the one who'd introduced them. Gary had been the instructor in a yoga class Madison had briefly taken for stress relief during med school.

"I didn't run Gary off," she muttered, looking around to make sure there were no eavesdroppers on this personal conversation. "He was looking for someone who was ready for a permanent commitment, and I wasn't interested in that then."

Nor would Gary have been the right one if she had been looking, she added silently.

"Then," Madison repeated quickly. "What about now? You're not getting any younger you know, sis."

"Thanks a lot."

"You should call Seth. Let him know you're interested, even if you're busy. And you really should see about cutting back on your work schedule a little. You're not a resident anymore, you know. You've got a good start in your career. You can make time for a life outside the hospital, and you should. Am I right, Mom?"

Still looking distracted, their mother nodded. "I hope all my children find loving partners eventually, who'll make you as happy as I was with your father. And I would like to have grandchildren eventually," she added with a faint smile. "Maybe I shouldn't have raised you girls to be quite so independent and career minded."

Meagan reached out to gently squeeze her mother's arm. "You raised us just fine, Mom."

"Thank you, sweetie. Let's go check on your grandmother now."

Knowing there would be no delaying her further, Meagan agreed. At least her mom had some color in her face again. The coffee break had served its purpose.

Walking with them, Madison met Meagan's eyes behind their mother's back. "Call Seth," she mouthed.

With a sigh, Meagan looked away, lamely pretending she hadn't received the message.

It was past eight when Meagan got home Sunday evening. As she'd expected, her mother had insisted on staying at the hospital. Meagan knew her mom would be comfortable enough in the foldout bed the hospital provided in each private room for family members. Not that anyone slept particularly well in a hospital room, but it would have been a waste of breath to try to send her mom home that night. Maybe tomorrow night she'd agree to go home for awhile, if Meemaw was doing better.

As was her habit, Meagan laid out her clothes for the next day and then brewed a mug of hot tea to help her relax for the remainder of the evening until bedtime. There wasn't much on TV to interest her and she couldn't concentrate on reading, so she caught up on some busywork on her computer for an hour or so. At just before ten she found herself at a front window in her living room, gazing at the house just down the street. Lights burned in windows both upstairs and downstairs, so it looked as though the occupants hadn't yet turned in.

Call Seth. She could still clearly picture her sister's face as she had mouthed the command.

Should she? Was she being rude by not calling? Maybe he'd been waiting for her to make the next move, since he'd done all the calling before. Maybe it had been so long since she'd been active in the dating scene that she had forgotten some of the "rules."

She glanced at her watch. Still ten minutes before ten. That wasn't too late for a quick call, was it?

Her hand was actually a little unsteady when she picked up her phone. How silly of her. She was a skilled surgeon whose hands could slice neatly through skin and muscle and reattach tiny blood vessels and nerve endings. Why on earth would a simple phone call unnerve her?

Seth had checked his caller ID when he answered. "Hi, Meagan."

"Hi. I hope it's not too late to call."

"Not at all. Everything's okay with you, I hope."

"I've spent most of the day today at the hospital with my

mom and grandmother. My grandmother has been admitted for an infection, but I'm pretty confident she'll be able to go home again in a few days."

"I'm sorry to hear she's ill again. Is there anything I can do for you?"

"No, thanks, everything's under control. I was just, um, wondering how you and Alice are."

"We're fine, thanks for asking. Busy. You know."

"Yes. I know." She moistened her lips. "And Jacqui? Still working out for you?"

"Yeah. We're settling into a routine with her. No complaints. By the way, she was startled to find out she'd been initially interviewed for this job by a surgeon. For some reason, it bothered her that she didn't call you Dr. Baker during the interview."

Meagan laughed. "That was hardly necessary."

"That's what I told her, but she seems to have a very high regard for doctors. I think she'd have been more intimidated by you if she'd known at the time what you do."

"Odd. Next time I see her, I'll try to put her at ease."

A brief silence followed her light remark. She wondered if Seth, like herself, was wondering if there would be any occasion for her to see Jacqui again.

"I haven't seen any evidence that Alice has used the pool during the past week," she said a bit too quickly. "You did tell her she's welcome, didn't you?"

"I did. But she's been in the pool almost every afternoon with her swim team, so I guess she's getting enough swim time in. She said it wouldn't be as much fun at your house without you there, anyway."

Meagan doubted that he'd intended to make her feel guilty that she hadn't been available for the girl—but she did, anyway. "I'm home some weekends, but I was on call yesterday and busy with my grandmother today."

"You have a very busy life."

"Yes. You met me at a time when I just happened to be temporarily sidelined."

"I'm figuring that out."

There were so many undercurrents beneath the seemingly casual conversation that she couldn't begin to interpret them all. "Normally it's not quite as bad as this past week has been. Trying to catch up from my time off."

"I can imagine how far behind I'd be after a month away from the office. Must be hectic."

"Exactly." Maybe he did understand. Maybe she was only imagining disapproval in his voice. "When does Alice leave for her big trip?"

"Friday after next."

She knew she wasn't imagining the dread she heard in him. He would miss Alice terribly. "I'd love to see her before she leaves."

"I'm sure she'd like to see you, too. Not sure when you're going to get together, though, with both your busy schedules. Next weekend is booked solid for her. Her swim team has a meet Saturday, the last one she'll get to participate in for a month. They're having a big family cookout afterward. Her grandparents want to see her before she leaves, too, so I promised we'd drive up for a visit Sunday afternoon."

"I see." She had hoped there would be a little time next weekend for her to spend with Alice, but it sounded as though that wasn't going to happen. "What about some evening this week? I could probably arrange to be home by seven on whichever evening she's free. I know you and she will have already eaten dinner by then, but maybe she— and you, too, if you like—could come over for dessert?"

"She'd probably like to have you all to herself. How does Thursday sound? As far as I know, there's nothing on her schedule Thursday evening."

"Oh." She kept her voice deliberately breezy. "That would be lovely. I'll keep Thursday evening open. Will you extend the invitation or should I call her and ask if she wants to come over?"

"I'll tell her, and I'm sure she'll want to come. She's asked about you several times."

"Thursday, then. Either of you can call me if anything comes up in the meantime. And if you change your mind about joining us, the invitation stands."

"Thanks, Meagan."

It didn't sound as if he intended to change his mind. For some reason, Seth was pulling back, and he wasn't being particularly subtle about it. "All right. Good night, Seth."

"Good night. Thanks for calling."

"Good night, Seth." But he'd already hung up.

So much for Madison's determined matchmaking, Meagan thought as she tossed the phone aside and rose to prepare for bed. There would be no future for her and Seth. It had taken only one week of her back at work for Seth to reach the same conclusion as Gary, apparently. She worked too much, was too involved in her career, wasn't available enough for him—or maybe Seth was more worried that she wasn't available enough for Alice. A very legitimate concern, she had to admit, and the reason she'd said all along that she shouldn't get involved with a single dad.

At least she could say she'd given it a shot. She'd been open to the idea of a relationship for the first time in quite a while. She'd been prepared to make some changes, to work out some compromises that would allow her more free time without sacrificing her commitment to her patients. So Seth had just been the wrong man at the right time. All she needed now was to find the right one, as her mother had said.

Unfortunately, it had felt so very right when she'd been in Seth's arms. She couldn't imagine finding that feeling again anytime soon with anyone else.

Chapter Nine

Because he didn't want Alice to catch him peering out the window, Seth was deliberately immersed in work in his home office when she returned from Meagan's house at the agreed-upon time Thursday evening. He'd heard the front door open, heard Alice calling out goodbyes to Meagan, who had either watched to make sure she had arrived safely or walked her home. He'd heard the door slam and the locks click and Alice's quick steps in the hallway, though he tried to look as though he hadn't been craning his ears toward all those sounds when she popped up in the doorway.

He glanced away from his computer, pushing aside a thick folder of reports. "Oh. You're home. Did you have a good time?"

"Yes. And you would have had a good time, too, if you hadn't been such a stick in the mud and refused to go."

So she was still pouting about that. He'd thought she'd appreciate having a couple of hours alone with her friend, but she'd tried her best to talk him into joining her and Meagan for dessert.

"I told you, I had work to do."

"It could have waited."

He couldn't honestly dispute that. The work could have waited. And he hadn't been all that noble in allowing Alice one-on-one time with Meagan. Truth was, his resistance had been more self-serving. He had suspected it would be too difficult for him to spend even a couple of hours that close to Meagan without wanting to touch her. To kiss her again. Knowing the odds were slim he would ever do either again.

It would have been almost as hard to watch Alice chatting so happily with her friend, gazing at Meagan with her usual adoring admiration. He worried still that Alice would be hurt by this unconventional friendship. Meagan herself had admitted that it had begun under unusual circumstances, that her true life bore little resemblance to the weeks in which Alice and Seth had gotten to know her.

But Alice had Jacqui to befriend now, he reminded himself. The two had gotten along great during Alice's first week off from school, with Jacqui starting the knitting lessons and chauffeuring Alice to swim classes and taking her shopping for a few things for the upcoming trip. The trip itself should be another way of distancing Alice from Meagan. Alice would love spending that time with her mother, whom she had missed so much during the past six months. She wouldn't need a substitute then.

As for himself…well, he'd stay very busy while Alice was gone. Maybe he'd even take advantage of being a single adult again and go out some. He could always call Susan.

He tried not to remember Alice sticking a finger down her throat at the mention of Susan's name.

"What did Meagan serve you for dessert?"

"The yummiest chocolate meringue cake. Oh my gosh, it was so good! It was filled with something she called ganache, and it was the best stuff ever. We had hot tea with it, decaf with milk and sugar in mine."

He could almost feel his mouth watering for a slice of the cake his daughter had just described. He had a particular weakness for chocolate cake. "Sounds great."

"It was. Meagan didn't make it herself, she picked it up at a bakery on the way home because she said she didn't really have time to make anything, but that didn't matter. I know she's busy. We both loved it and we had a great time talking and laughing."

Alice had probably enjoyed the bakery dessert as much as she would have liked something home cooked, Seth conceded. The conversation and attention from Meagan had meant much more to her.

Seth stood and stretched, speaking in what he hoped was a casual tone. "So what did you girls talk about?"

"I asked her a lot of questions about being a surgeon. She said she didn't mind me asking. She told me a lot of funny stories about things that happen in the O.R.—that's what they call the operating rooms—and some of her funny patients, though she said she couldn't use any names because of HIPAA laws. Do you know what that means?"

"Yes, I'm familiar with patient privacy laws." He resisted the impulse to remind her that he was an attorney, after all.

"Oh, well, anyway, she taught me a lot. Do you know what ERCP stands for?"

"Uh, no, I can't say I do."

"Endoscopic retrograde cholangiopancreatography." She recited the words carefully and a bit smugly, that she had known something he hadn't. "Meagan told me about it. It's a diagnostic procedure that uses a scope and X-rays to find problems in the liver, gallbladder, pancreas and... um, something else. Oh, yeah, the bile ducts."

"How on earth did that come up in your conversation?"

"I was asking some of the ways surgeons find out what's wrong with people so they'll know what to operate on and that was one of the tests she said they use a lot. She said I could impress my friends by knowing what the letters stand for."

He smiled wryly. "I'm sure you will."

"If I can remember it." She repeated the words beneath her breath, committing them more firmly to her memory.

"Changing your mind about becoming a surgeon?"

"I still think I want to be an orthodontist. But I'm not ruling anything out," Alice quipped.

"That's good. Keep your options open."

She gazed up at him, and her expression was suddenly so mature it took him aback. She'd been wearing contacts for the past three days, and combined with her new hairstyle, she looked older than the little girl he still thought her. "Why didn't you want to go tonight, Dad? Why did Meagan look funny when we talked about you? Actually, she wouldn't talk about you much at all. She kept changing the subject. Did the two of you have an argument or something?"

"No, of course not. I told you, Alice, I had work to do."

She frowned in disapproval at the prevarication. "It could have waited," she said again.

He tugged at one of her curls, as he'd done when she was little and a simple, "Because Daddy said so," was enough to satisfy her. "Just enjoy your friendship with Meagan, okay, sweetheart? That's enough for now, isn't it?"

"You seemed to really like her."

"I do like her. But I also warned you against matchmaking. This just isn't the time for that—not that any time is right for you to try to fix me up," he added. "You're going to have to leave that sort of thing to me."

"If I leave it up to you, you'll be an old man with a walker next time you get a date," she muttered.

He couldn't help laughing. "Hey! That's not quite true."

"Oh, right. Susan."

Alice raised a hand, obviously intended to do her gagging routine again, but Seth caught her arm to forestall her. "I'm through working for tonight. I think I'll have a cup of tea or something before bed."

Even that random comment reminded him of Meagan, but he pushed the thought away. He would focus on his daughter—his little girl, despite her maturing appearance—for what was left of the evening. He had so little time left with her in the next few weeks—not to mention the rest of her life, he thought with philosophical wistfulness.

She wrapped both her arms around his right arm. "Maybe you'd like a little something to go with that cup of tea?"

"Yeah?" Walking with her toward the hallway, he turned off the office light behind them. "Like what?"

"Like the big slice of chocolate meringue cake—with yummy ganache—I brought you from Meagan's house."

His mouth started tingling again. "You brought me cake?"

Alice laughed. "Meagan insisted I bring you some. It was her idea. I left it on the hall table. But of course, if it's too much of a commitment for you to eat a slice of her cake…"

"Brat."

Alice giggled again and hugged his arm.

This, he thought in satisfaction, was enough. He had his daughter, his work—and a big slice of chocolate cake waiting for him. He was a very lucky man. Why should it feel as though there was still something missing in his life?

Two weeks after her visit with Alice, Meagan turned her car onto her street at just before seven o'clock. It was nice to be home a little earlier than usual. It was still quite light on this second week in June. Maybe she'd have dinner by the pool, maybe have a swim afterward.

The thought of her pool almost made her sigh. It would seem very quiet in her backyard by herself. She would almost welcome Waldo's company.

Thirty minutes later, she sat at her patio table with a salad made of mixed greens topped with rotisserie chicken and mandarin oranges and drizzled with balsamic dressing. She had a glass of iced tea and a handful of whole-grain crackers to accompany the salad, and frozen yogurt bars for dessert later. She had changed out of her work clothes and into a sleek bathing suit topped with a short, sleeveless black cover-up with white piping. Flirty black flip-flops studded with faux jewels protected her bare feet from the sun-warmed, tinted concrete that made up the patio. Perhaps there was no one around to admire her appearance, but she'd dressed to please herself, thinking the sporty outfit would help lighten her inexplicably melancholy mood.

She wasn't sad, she assured herself. Nor angry, nor particularly unhappy. She was just a little blue, and that happened to everyone at times, right? She was sure this lovely salad, followed by a leisurely evening swim, would be just the pick-me-up she needed.

She had just spread a yellow linen napkin over her lap when her attention was captured by a sound coming from the other side of the redwood gate that closed off her backyard. The gate was locked, she reminded herself. She was safe inside the enclosure—especially since her kitchen door was only a few leaps away, if necessary.

Something scratched again at the gate, and this time the sound was accompanied by a series of eager, demanding barks. Familiar barks, she realized with a groan. Quickly setting her napkin aside, she rushed to unlock the gate.

The moment he had an opening, Waldo pushed his way inside, leaping toward her, trying to reach her face for a slobbery lick-kiss. She caught him in midair, pushing downward. He'd grown considerably in the past couple of months, and was too big for her to carry easily now—not that carrying him had been easy the last time. "Down, Waldo. Sit."

Showing off his obedience school training—which obviously only extended so far—he sat dutifully on the grass, tail wagging behind him, mouth spread in a big doggie grin. He barked once, as though demanding praise that he'd complied so well with her instruction.

"Good boy," she said, then realized that she was the one performing on command. "How on earth did you get out of your fence again?"

But he wasn't sharing that secret. He merely reached out to lick her hand, still sitting restlessly at her feet.

She knew Alice wasn't home. She couldn't tell by looking across the street whether Seth was there. She supposed there was only one way to find out. Taking a firm grasp on Waldo's leather collar with her left hand, she stepped out of her backyard and closed the gate behind her with her right hand, leaving it unlocked since she didn't intend to be gone long.

"Okay, Waldo, walk. Uh, heel."

He tugged a little against her tight hold, but she didn't let him get away. This would have been much easier with a leash, she thought, bending sideways to lead him down the driveway to the street. Fortunately there were no cars passing just then, so she was able to guide him across. He didn't resist, which was a good thing. She pictured herself dragging him the rest of the way and grimaced in response to the ridiculous image.

Finally standing at Seth's front door, she told Waldo to sit, which he did on the second repetition. "Stay," she added, though she kept a grip on his collar while she reached up to press the doorbell.

He whined, but didn't attempt an escape, to her relief.

She rang the bell a second time, then waited several moments before conceding in frustration that no one was inside.

Now what? She could put Waldo back into the fence, if the gate wasn't locked, but he'd probably just get out again through the same escape route he'd used earlier. She supposed she'd have to take him back home with her and keep him inside her own fence until Seth came to collect him. She would call Seth as soon as...

But that thought was interrupted when Seth's car turned into the driveway.

"That's a relief," she muttered, waving to make sure he saw her standing there as the garage door rose. Waldo lunged toward the car, but she managed to hold on to him, staggering a little before regaining her balance. "Sit!"

She almost imagined she heard a reluctant sigh from the mutt before he plopped his wriggling butt back down on the porch.

Moments later, Seth rounded the corner of the house to join them. "Don't tell me he got out again."

"I'm afraid so. I found him at my gate."

"I hope you haven't been waiting here long."

"No, only a couple of minutes. I was just about to call you."

"Thanks for rescuing him again. I'm sorry he keeps doing this to you."

She smiled. "It's only the second time. I'm just glad he hasn't been hurt in one of his adventures."

"Me, too. Alice would be heartbroken. Here, let me take him." He reached out to grab the dog's collar, and his hand lay for a moment against Meagan's.

Their eyes met over the dog's head, hands freezing on the strap of leather. Meagan was suddenly, acutely aware of her bare arms and legs in contrast to the tailored suit and tie Seth still wore from work. His gaze wandered momentarily, and she imagined he'd studied every revealed inch of her in that brief survey.

Her cheeks warming, she released the collar and straightened rather abruptly, resisting an impulse to tug at the very short hem of her cover-up. "I wonder how he keeps getting out," she blurted.

Kneeling beside Waldo, Seth was now at eye level with her thighs. He cleared his throat. "I, um—not sure. I never found the way he got out last time. I just assumed Alice had left the gate open and it had swung closed behind him. It wasn't locked then, but I would have sworn I left it locked this morning."

"Maybe Jacqui left it unlocked, for some reason."

"Yeah. Maybe she did, though I can't imagine why she would have opened it. I'll check when I put him back inside the fence. And I'll do another walk-around to see if I can find a break anywhere he could be squeezing through. If I don't find anything, I'm putting him in the garage for the night and calling a fence service tomorrow to have a professional take a look. Can't risk the mutt getting hit by a car while Alice is gone."

There was no reason for her to stay, but she lingered a bit longer to ask, "How is Alice? Is she having a good time in Europe?"

"She's having a great time. She calls every day to tell me about everything she's done and seen. It sounds as though Colleen is making a real effort to show Alice a good time. They're really enjoying themselves."

"I'm glad. I'm sure it will be hard for them to say good-bye at the end of their month."

He shrugged. "Yeah. It'll be rough. But this is the life Colleen wants and Alice has accepted that, I think. She's a brave kid."

"She's very special. You've done a wonderful job raising her."

"Thanks." Though the single syllable was a bit gruff, she could tell he was pleased by the compliment. "I won't take all the credit. Colleen was much more involved in Alice's earliest years. She waited until she thought Alice was old enough to deal with it before she took off to pursue her own dreams."

This was hardly the time or place for a conversation about Alice's mother, Meagan told herself. She took a step toward the walkway. "Tell Alice I said hello, if you think about it. Good night, Seth."

"Thanks again for bringing Waldo home."

"You're welcome."

She walked down the steps, looking over her shoulder as she moved toward her own home. Something about the way Seth watched her leave made her steps falter a bit. He looked tired. And maybe a little lonely, or was she merely projecting that part? She could only imagine how much he missed his daughter.

"I was just going to eat a salad and take a swim," she said on an impulse she didn't try to resist. "Maybe you'd like to join me after you put Waldo away? I've always found swimming to be relaxing after a long day at work."

He seemed surprised by the invitation, but maybe a little intrigued, as well? She couldn't really tell.

Yet when he spoke, she could tell by his tone that he was going to decline. "Thanks, but I've already eaten. And I guess I'd better work on the fence tonight."

She nodded. "All right. Good luck with that. See you, Seth."

"See you, Meagan."

She didn't look back when she walked away, so she didn't know whether he watched her leave.

She made a very deliberate effort to enjoy her now-slightly-limp salad when she returned to her patio table. The shadows lengthened around her as the sun slid downward at just past eight o'clock. It had been an especially hot day for mid-June and the air was still quite warm, though a slight breeze rustled leaves and brushed like comforting fingertips against her cheeks. A scarlet cardinal cheeped in a branch overhead and ruby-throated hummingbirds chittered and fought around the feeder hanging outside her kitchen window.

She had vowed during her medical leave to make more time for herself, for relaxing and enjoying her life, taking better care of her health and welfare. As easy as it would have been to fall back into her former routine of overworking and overscheduling, she saw this evening as proof that she had changed her ways—at least a little. Her worried mother would be pleased if she saw her now. Which reminded her that she needed to call her mom after the swim.

And then she felt a little guilty because she knew her poor mother had little free time these days for relaxing by a pool.

Sighing, she told herself she was still getting the hang of this new "me-time" endeavor. She didn't seem to be very good at it yet. She was still fretting about the things she should be doing, instead.

She stood and stretched, her gaze on the clear, sparkling water of the blue-lined pool. A few hard laps, followed by a warm shower and a cup of hot tea, would complete the relaxation regime she had prescribed for herself that evening. After a few hours sleep, she'd be back at work at six-thirty in the morning, bright-eyed and re-energized and happy to be back in the life she loved.

Or so she hoped.

Tossing her cover-up over the back of a chair, she kicked off her sandals and descended the steps into the pool. The water was just the right temperature, closing around her in a warm welcome as she kicked away from the steps to begin the first lap. She wasn't trying to break any speed or endurance records. She swam in steady, even strokes from one end of the pool to the other, flipping and pushing away in practiced turns she had learned as a teenager.

She could have been on a swim team, she thought, her mind wandering as she sliced mechanically through the pool. She'd been a pretty good swimmer back then. But she'd been so focused on her studies in science and pre-medicine that she hadn't wanted to take the time it would have required to be truly competitive as an athlete. She was glad that Alice was having a more well-rounded youth. She gave Seth credit for...

But no. Her strokes faltered, and she dipped awkwardly beneath the water for a moment before shaking her head and restarting her laps. She wasn't going to think about

Seth any more tonight, she told herself fiercely, pumping her legs more furiously. Alice, either. This was her "me-time." She was going to enjoy it, darn it.

"Training for the Olympics?"

The wry question startled her so much that she stopped swimming—and promptly sank. She emerged sputtering, her heart pounding in alarm. "Wha—?"

Seth stood beside the pool, watching her with an expression on his face she couldn't begin to interpret.

He'd changed, she realized, dropping her feet to stand in the shallow end of the pool. He wore a gray T-shirt and a pair of black board shorts with casual, slip-on canvas shoes. A navy and white print beach towel was draped over one shoulder. He had come prepared to swim.

"You startled me," she admitted, wondering why he had changed his mind when he'd been so firm in declining her invitation.

He motioned behind him. "I was going to call out to you, but you left your gate unlocked. You shouldn't do that, you know. Anyone could have walked in and caught you off guard."

"I guess I forgot to lock it behind me when I came back in."

That was such an obvious comment that she almost winced at the inanity of it.

"Um—where's Waldo?" she blurted. And then wanted to sink beneath the water again at how foolish that sounded.

"He's having his dinner. I think I found the place where he got out of the yard—he'd dug a hole beneath the higher side of the fence, which gave him just enough of an opening to squeeze through. I've blocked it solidly enough for tonight, and I'll have someone come reinforce the bottom of the fence tomorrow."

He didn't seem to know what to do with his hands. He pushed them into the pockets of the loose shorts. "I, uh, hope you haven't changed your mind about me joining you. After I took care of Waldo, I decided a swim sounded pretty nice."

"The invitation still stands," she said quietly, meeting his eyes. "Come on in."

He hesitated only a moment before tossing a set of keys on the patio table and then tugging his T-shirt over his head. And even though Meagan stood in a pool of water, her hair dripping behind her, her face wet from her swim, her mouth went dry.

She'd seen glimpses of his chest that night they'd made out like eager teenagers on her couch. But this was the first time she'd seen him without a shirt. It was a sight worth waiting for.

Without looking away from her, he descended into the pool. She stood her ground, watching as he waded to join her.

Stopping very close to her, he looked down at her body in her modest, but formfitting black maillot. And then his gaze lifted to hers again. "Meagan—"

She wasn't sure who moved first. The water lapped against them as they melted into each other's arms.

He'd tried to resist. He'd told himself it wouldn't be fair to Meagan or himself to continue something that had little chance of success. He'd mentally argued that it was wrong to lead her on, when he had already come to the conclusion that there could be no real future for them. Even had he been looking for a permanent relationship—which he wasn't, not at this point in his and Alice's life—Meagan would not have been the obvious choice.

Hadn't he learned the hard way that two driven workaholics could not successfully integrate a meaningful and permanent relationship into their hectic schedules? Especially when a child was involved?

Lasting relationships required full-time effort. Compromises. Sacrifices. Commitments. The same things he was already giving his daughter and his career. He just wasn't sure he had anything left to give.

Except for tonight.

Remembering the way Meagan had looked at him when she'd invited him into the pool, he hoped that would be enough for her.

The kisses were hungry. Heated. But then slowed as both seemed to realize there was no need to rush. There was nothing else waiting for either of them just then. No one expecting anything from them.

They swam. Side by side, in long, matched strokes, sometimes pausing to laugh or splash. Or share a few more wet kisses. No racing or competing or dutifully counting laps, just swimming. Playing.

When was the last time he'd played with a woman? No kids, no dogs, just two healthy adults having a good time, enjoying each other and the moment. He couldn't even remember.

He refused to deliberately compare Meagan to Colleen. That wouldn't be fair to either of them. But he was only human, and he couldn't help thinking that Colleen had never been one to encourage adult play. If she was in a pool, it was for exercise, pushing herself to the limits of her endurance, taking satisfaction from going a little farther each time.

Pushing his ex-wife out of his mind, he focused on the woman in the water with him, instead.

Sensor-operated security lights turned on as the sunlight faded to lavender and then to gray. The lights lent a warm illumination to the area, but were dimmed enough that the effect was more intimate than glaring. He and Meagan were spending more time now exploring each other than swimming. Kisses had become deep, penetrating embraces. Teasing touches slowed into long, arousing strokes. Their bodies came together, legs entwining beneath the surface of the water. Pressing Meagan against the side of the pool, Seth supported them when she wrapped her legs around his waist, her fingers clenched on his shoulders as he plunged his tongue deep into her warm, welcoming mouth.

Secure within the privacy of her tall fence, he slipped her bathing suit straps from her shoulders, lowering the top slowly down her arms. He lifted her higher against the side of the pool, lowering his head to taste the creamy, wet flesh he'd uncovered. Meagan made a soft sound of pleasure and encouragement and arched to meet him. She moved rhythmically against his straining erection, drawing a groan from his throat.

When she pushed against his shoulders, he almost groaned again. If she was calling a halt at this point, he knew he was in for a long, painfully sleepless night ahead. Considering the circumstances, he could understand her hesitation to carry this to the natural conclusion. He wouldn't protest, wouldn't try to change her mind—but damn, he would suffer.

She drew a deep, shuddering breath, as though trying to regain enough air to sustain her voice. And then she gave him a smile that made his knees threaten to buckle.

"Maybe we should take this inside before we both drown," she murmured.

At that moment, the risk of drowning seemed a very minor concern. It would almost be worth it, he thought, studying her floating so unselfconsciously in front of him.

But then he returned her smile and held out his hand. "Lead the way."

Without bothering to straighten her suit, she turned and waded toward the pool steps, her fingers laced with his.

Chapter Ten

"Darn it, McCallum, either hold the retractors out of the way or give them to someone else."

"Sorry, Dr. Baker." The medical student straightened sharply, focusing on her task of holding tissue out of the way so Meagan could complete the bowel resection currently underway. They'd been at it for five hours, but she had no sympathy for the third-year medical student whose job was simply to hold the retractors.

"And watch that left arm. You break the sterile field at this point, I'll break your fingers."

The student laughed nervously when the others gathered around the draped patient chuckled in response to Meagan's only half teasing threat. They'd all heard it before. Every medical student had accidentally contaminated the sterile field—known as "the blue field" in the O.R.—at some point, but doing so always resulted in a stern censure from the surgeon, scrub tech or resident. Sometimes from all of them at once.

Once the surgical team was scrubbed in, their arms could never drop below waist level, nor could they touch anything outside the sterile field without having to scrub out and then scrub back in. Most infractions were minor, but occasionally an entire tray of sterilized surgical tools had to be replaced, or even worse, a patient recovered in sterile blue drapes. Either of those could result in a tantrum from the surgeon or the scrub tech, most of whom were fiercely protective of their fields.

"Light," Meagan said, and her first assistant, an upper-level resident, hurriedly repositioned the sterile-draped articulated light pointed at the area where Meagan was working.

Meagan figured in about another half hour she could step aside and let the eager resident close. She heard her cell phone beep to indicate she'd received a text message. Well out of the sterile area, the phone rested on a counter at the far side of the operating room. Looking over the mask that covered the lower half of her face, she glanced around at one of the "floater" nurses who stood outside the sterile periphery. "Mind reading that message for me?"

It wasn't an unusual request. Considering her grandmother's precarious health, Meagan didn't like to ignore messages unless she had to. The nurse, one Meagan had worked with numerous times in the past couple of years, punched a couple of buttons on the phone. A moment later, she said, "Someone named Seth said he's sorry, but he'll be about an hour late for dinner. He said send him a text back if you need to reply."

Not an emergency, then. Meagan relaxed and turned her attention back to her patient. "Thanks, Kathy."

"You're welcome, Dr. Baker."

"Steady," Meagan warned the med student, whose concentration appeared to be wandering again. The young woman snapped back into position.

This one wouldn't make a surgeon even had she wanted to become one, Meagan thought with a slight shake of her head. She had the attention span of a gnat.

"So, Seth, huh?" Gale, the scrub tech and one of Meagan's favorite coworkers, eyed her with a teasing smile crinkling the part of her brown face exposed by her surgical mask. "That's not a name I've heard from you before. Someone you met while you were on vacation?"

"It was hardly a vacation," Meagan replied without glancing up from her suturing. "I was recuperating from surgery, remember?"

"Someone you met while recuperating from surgery?" Gale asked, refusing to be sidetracked.

"A neighbor."

"Single neighbor?"

"I wouldn't be having dinner with a married neighbor. Well, not just with him—oh, you know what I mean."

The medical student looked with rounded eyes from Gale to Meagan and back again, but no one else paid much attention to the joking. A couple of other discussions were taking place around them, underscored by the soft rock music Meagan preferred listening to while she worked.

"I'm going to want details, you know, especially if you're getting serious with some dude."

Meagan glanced up from the bowel long enough to wink at the scrub tech. "You know I'm not one to kiss and tell, Gale."

Gale laughed. "So, there is something to tell?"

Shaking her head with exaggerated regret, Meagan heaved a sigh. "No. He's a cutie, but a single dad. You know how that goes."

"Uh-huh. Dr. Baker's famous rules of engagement." Having tried once unsuccessfully to arrange a blind date between Meagan and a divorced friend with a couple of kids, Gale knew exactly how Meagan had always felt about getting involved with single dads.

"Hey, they've worked for me so far." Meagan nodded toward the resident to adjust the light another fraction and bent over her work again.

Gale started to continue the teasing, but then whirled toward the beleaguered medical student.

"Watch that arm!" she snapped, protecting her imperiled blue field like a guard dog on patrol. "Didn't Dr. Baker just tell you to keep that left arm up?"

"Sorry," the young woman muttered, shifting her weight uncomfortably in the awkward position she had maintained for most of the past five hours.

Stripping off her mask and gloves, her phone stowed now in the pocket of her scrubs, Meagan left the O.R. twenty minutes later. The very capable resident was closing, which made the med student first assistant for the next few minutes. Heaven help them all.

She thought she'd handled Gale's teasing about Seth well enough, keeping it light, making it sound as though this was nothing more than a passing flirtation. Which, of course, she supposed it was, since neither she nor Seth had made any reference to the future during the days that had passed since he'd joined her in the pool—and in her bed.

They had been together four times since then, mostly on weekends when they both had a little more free time. She had enjoyed every minute she'd spent with him. They'd laughed and talked, swam and played her favorite word game at her house, avoiding the blazing heat that had come with July. They'd rented a couple of movies and snuggled in his den with popcorn and sodas. And they'd made love. Oh, had they made love.

Yet in all those lovely hours together, they had not once talked of anything particularly important. They mentioned Alice, of course, more in the context of how she was enjoying her travels than any talk of when she would return. They shared a few funny anecdotes from their pasts—high school, college, law school and med school—but no speculation about their futures, separate or otherwise.

Though they weren't hiding out, exactly, they didn't go out in public, nor did they invite other people in. Perhaps neither wanted to share the other's attention. At least, that was the way Meagan felt. They made loose plans—such as for tonight's dinner—but nothing more than a few days ahead. And nothing at all beyond Alice's return in just under two weeks.

She told herself that was fine. If all she and Seth had was another two weeks, more or less, then they would make the most of those two weeks. For two weeks, she could make a little extra time in her schedule to spend with him. Get home a little earlier once in a while, as he seemed to be trying to do for her, despite whatever had come up today. And when the two weeks ended Seth could concentrate completely on his job and his daughter again and she would renew her commitment to her own career, both of them refreshed and recharged from their virtual vacation together.

A passing flirtation. Nothing more.

That was what she wanted everyone to believe, anyway. Including herself.

During the next seven days, Seth had to cancel plans they'd made once when something came up at work. Meagan had to cancel once and was called away by her mother just as they were sitting down to dinner another time. On the second Tuesday in July, only four days before Alice was due home on Saturday, they finally managed to eat an entire meal at her place. Both were exhausted after a particularly long, demanding day at their jobs, so they had a late dinner of Chinese takeout Meagan had picked up on the way home.

Since Alice had left for her trip, Seth had told Jacqui there was no need for her to cook dinners, letting her leave a little earlier each evening. He'd fended for himself when he or Meagan had other plans, and joined her for quick meal preparations or takeout when they were both available.

"Don't take this the wrong way," Seth said, eyeing her across the dinner table. "But you look wiped out."

She smiled faintly. "No offense taken. I guess I am a little tired tonight. I did a routine, hour-long procedure at seven this morning, then started an operation that should have taken about five hours but that ended up taking eight, instead. Complications. And I still had another forty-five minute procedure and rounds to do after that. A little more hectic than usual."

He frowned in sympathy. "Did the patient survive? The one with complications?"

"Yes, though it'll be touch and go for the next twenty-four hours. I'm cautiously optimistic about his full recovery."

"Eight hours." He shook his head. "On your feet that entire time bent over a patient?"

"I don't really have to bend over. We position the patient to give me comfortable access. Some operations take even longer than that one."

"So during those long operations do you—uh, take breaks? You know, if you have to?"

"Let's just say I don't drink a lot of liquids before surgery in the mornings," she explained with a smile, having encountered this question before. "I can descrub during an operation if I have to, then scrub back in as soon as possible afterward. It's not as though the patient is left without care if I take a ten-minute break. There are assistants—resident and med student, an anesthesiologist, nurses and the scrub tech—all available as needed. But I try not to leave during a procedure unless it is necessary."

"I can tell comfortable shoes are a must for your job."

"No kidding. And we're provided good rubber mats to stand on—unlike the med students who usually have to stand on a hard stool in a very uncomfortable position to hold retractors or whatever else we need them to do," she added wryly. "I was just glad I didn't have McCallum holding the retractor—a third-year med student rotating through surgery this month. She's got a reputation for letting her mind wander. I had to snap at her several times during surgery last week and I heard Dr. Bellsmith threw one of his famous tantrums in her direction."

"Ouch. That sounds painful."

"Trust me, it is. I was the lucky recipient of one of those tantrums when I was an intern and made a stupid mistake."

"A mistake? You? Don't believe it."

She chuckled. "I've made my share."

"We had this professor in law school—Dr. Szabo—man, could he yell. He had a reputation for throwing out random questions totally unrelated to anything he happened to be lecturing about, and if you didn't instantly produce the answer he wanted you could expect to be called an idiot and a poseur who should be cleaning toilets rather than studying law. And that was if he was in a good mood."

She laughed softly. "That sounds like the voice of experience."

He grinned. "I've made my share of mistakes, too."

It was nice sitting there in her dining room, the lights dimmed, candles flickering between them, instrumental music playing softly from a hidden speaker. She'd figured the least she could do since they were having takeout was to arrange a nice atmosphere in which to enjoy it. Especially since they'd been able to enjoy so few of these moments together. And had so few left to share.

Their gazes met and she spent a moment admiring the way the candlelight flickered in his green eyes, turning them to glittering emeralds. He reached out to place a hand over hers on the table, his thumb rubbing gently against her skin. "When I said you looked tired? Doesn't mean you aren't still beautiful."

Was he still worried that he had offended her with the observation? She resisted the impulse to argue that she wasn't beautiful, which would have sounded like fishing for compliments, and settled for a simple, "Thank you."

And then she quickly changed the subject. "Can I get you anything else? More tea? Something for dessert?"

"I'm good, thanks."

He still held her hand. She turned her wrist so that their fingers interlaced. "Then what would you like to do for the rest of the evening?" she asked with a little smile. "A swim, maybe? Some TV?"

Standing, he drew her to her feet and into his arms. "I'm sure we'll think of something to pass the time," he murmured, his mouth hovering just over hers.

She wrapped her arms around his neck and rose on tiptoes to brush her lips lightly, teasingly against his. "I'm sure we—"

They groaned in unison when the buzz of a phone cut off her words. It wasn't hers, she realized, grateful that she wasn't responsible for the interruption this time.

"I'm sorry." Seth grimaced as he drew the buzzing device from his pocket.

She turned to start clearing the table. "No problem. You can take the call in the living room if you like."

Nodding apologetically, he held the phone to his ear as he left the room. "Hello?"

Moments later, she heard him say in a raised voice, "Are you kidding me? At this hour?" And she knew their evening was over.

When he rejoined her a few minutes later, she might have considered his sheepish expression rather adorable had she not been so disappointed.

"I'm sorry," he said again.

"You have to go."

He nodded. "I would have refused if it hadn't been so important. A problem with one of the firm's biggest clients. Some reports that have to be filed by eight o'clock tomorrow morning and it turns out they weren't completed when I thought they were, so I guess I have to—"

"You don't have to explain, Seth," she interrupted gently. "Go. Take care of your client. At least we got to finish dinner this time."

His mouth twisted in what was probably intended to be a smile, but ended up being a regretful grimace. "This wasn't the way I wanted the evening to end."

"I know."

"Maybe tomorrow we can—?"

This time she was the one forced to express regrets. "I have a dinner with the chief of surgery. It could last rather late."

"Thursday, then."

"I'm on call Thursday night, but I'll be home unless I'm needed at the hospital."

"Then we'll plan to get together then—and to stay close to your phone."

She nodded. "Sounds good."

And after Thursday, there would be only one evening before Alice's return, she thought with a painful swallow. For Seth's sake, she was glad the time was passing so quickly before Alice was back home again. But if she were being strictly selfish, she would make those days pass a little more slowly, giving her a few more evenings to pretend she and Seth had all the time in the world together.

He kissed her lingeringly before moving reluctantly back. "I'll talk to you later."

"Good night, Seth. I hope you get some sleep tonight."

The look he gave her held a world of frustration. "I doubt I'll be sleeping very well tonight, no matter how long these reports take," he muttered, then spun and walked away almost angrily.

Knowing that anger wasn't directed toward her, Meagan sighed softly, then turned to blow out the candles still flickering on her table.

Glittering in the softened lighting, water streamed from Meagan's slender body as she climbed the steps out of the pool Friday evening. The red suit she wore fit like a second skin, molded around her wet curves. Seth lingered in the pool behind her, the better to watch her shapely backside as she bent to shake water from her hair. He watched in regret when she wrapped a thick towel around herself. Only then did he wade toward the steps, himself.

It was late, almost eleven, but he wasn't particularly sleepy, despite a killer day at the office. The stress of work had started seeping out of him as soon as Meagan had opened her door to him a few hours earlier, and had dissipated further during a leisurely meal. The lovemaking that had followed that had left him loose-limbed and satiated. Because neither had wanted to sleep afterward, they'd agreed on a quiet swim, which he, for one, had enjoyed very much.

Somewhat miraculously, not once during the evening had a phone rang—neither his nor hers. They'd managed only an hour together last night before Meagan had been called to the hospital for an emergency surgery, which had made tonight's uninterrupted time together even more special.

He ran a towel over his dripping head, swiped it over his chest, then looped it around his neck. "Getting tired?" he asked Meagan.

"I should be," she said with a smile. "It's been a long day. But for some reason, I'm not. I think I'd like a cup of tea. Do you want some?"

"Sounds good."

Sliding his damp, bare feet into his shoes, he followed her into the house.

Meagan took a quick shower and dressed quickly in a loose T-shirt and dorm pants. She left Seth to shower and dress while she went to make their tea. Only a few minutes later, dressed now in a polo shirt and jeans, he leaned against the kitchen doorway, watching her puttering around the kitchen. Two steaming mugs waited on the counter while she put away the tea canister and rummaged in the cupboard, maybe looking for a late-night snack to go with the hot beverage.

He could end every day just like this, he thought in a somewhat wistful satisfaction. If only Alice were here, everything would be perfect.

"Meagan."

She glanced over her shoulder with a distracted smile. "Yes?"

"Do you have plans for tomorrow?"

She shrugged and turned her attention back to the cupboard. "Nothing specific. I'm not on call, which doesn't mean my phone won't ring at some point, anyway, but I shouldn't have to go by the hospital. I need to do some laundry and grocery shopping, run by Mom's for a while, that sort of thing."

"Do you want to go with me to meet Alice at the airport?"

Her hands went still. He knew she hadn't missed the implications beneath the seemingly casual invitation.

"I'm sure you'd rather greet your daughter privately," she said after a moment, her voice oddly strained. "You haven't seen her in a month."

"She'd love to see you, too. She's asked about you several times when she called."

"You haven't told her we've been, um, seeing each other, have you?"

"No. I gave her the impression I've seen you in passing a few times. I didn't think she needed to know more than that. Yet."

She turned slowly, her expression troubled. "There's no need for her to ever know. We've had some fun. Spent a little free time together while you were at loose ends for a few weeks. That doesn't mean—"

He felt his eyebrows draw downward. "Are you suggesting I was using you to keep me from missing my daughter?"

"I never thought you were using me," she assured him hastily. "I've had a great time, too."

He didn't like the way she was using the past tense. Or the implication that their good times ended tonight.

He supposed he couldn't blame her for the way she had interpreted his actions during the past few weeks. Maybe at the beginning he had seen their evenings together as a temporary diversion. But the more time he spent with her, the more he wanted to be with her. He found himself wanting to believe they could still spend time together even after his life returned to normal.

"All I'm suggesting is that you come with me to get Alice."

"I know." She moistened her lips. "But I wouldn't want her to misinterpret us coming together to pick her up."

"Misinterpret in what way?" he asked, though he was pretty sure he got the idea.

"I don't want her to think we're a couple. Or even a potential couple. I want her to continue thinking of us as friends. Neighbors. Nothing more."

"Look, Meagan." He pushed a hand through his hair, wondering how to phrase what he wanted to say. "I think maybe I hurt your feelings a few weeks ago. I mean, we went out a couple of times, seemed to be hitting it off pretty well and then…well, I pulled back. I'll admit it. I started having second thoughts."

She opened her mouth to speak, but he forestalled her with a raised hand. "I guess I got a little nervous. Alice was matchmaking, everyone kept saying what a great couple we made, everything was going so well…and then you went back to work. And things, well, things changed."

He knew how awkward he sounded, but he didn't know how else to explain his behavior of the past month. He was still struggling to understand it, himself. He supposed he'd panicked a little when he'd realized how hard he was falling for his pretty neighbor. But in the long run, he just couldn't stay away. And the past three weeks had been amazing.

"Yes, things changed," Meagan repeated quietly.

He couldn't read her expression, and that made him uneasy. "It was my fault. I guess I started having flashbacks to my disastrous marriage with Colleen. We were a couple of workaholics who had no clue how to compromise. We were too young, too inflexible and too poorly suited to make it work out anyway. But it wasn't just career conflicts that broke us up—hell, we should never have gotten married in the first place. One failed attempt with the wrong woman doesn't mean I can't ever have a successful relationship with the right one, even as a single dad, as long as I keep Alice's welfare a top priority."

"The last thing I would ever want is for Alice to be hurt."

"You would never hurt Alice." That was one statement he could make with total certainty.

"No. I wouldn't."

"So, there's really no reason you and I can't keep seeing each other after she gets home. I mean, I know it will be even trickier to coordinate our schedules when we add her calendar, but—"

"There is one reason."

He hesitated, not sure he wanted to ask, but knowing he had to. "What?"

"I don't date men with children."

He blinked. "Uh—what?"

She grimaced in what might have been apology. "It's been a rule of mine for a long time. I sort of broke that rule when I went to the charity thing with you and I've broken it with you a few times since. While Alice was away, it was sort of a nonissue, but now that she's coming home—well, like I said. I don't date men with children."

"But these past few weeks…"

"I thought we were just having fun. Filling time."

"Filling time." He didn't like the way the words felt on his tongue.

"We can still be friends, of course."

He narrowed his eyes at her. "Let's avoid the clichés, shall we? I thought you liked Alice."

"I'm very fond of Alice. I think she's a great kid."

"But you won't go out with me because of her."

"I think that's for the best."

Her hands were clenched in front of her, her knuckles white. Had he not seen those signs, he would have thought she was perfectly at ease judging from her tone when she said, "You were right to pull back when you did, Seth. Now that Alice is coming home there's no place for me in your life now except perhaps as a friend. I understand that, and I agree."

"I don't agree," he insisted. "We've got a good thing going between us, Meagan. You and Alice already get along great. I know it won't be easy, considering everything, but…"

She was already shaking her head. "I'm sorry. This is just a bad time for me. I'm still catching up from my time off, my family's going through a difficult time and a new rotation will start soon with new residents and med students for me to teach. Summer brings vacations, which means extra work and call for everyone. There's just no time left for anything else."

"If there's one thing I've learned in the past thirteen years, it's that it's possible to make time for the things that are truly important to you," he said quietly. "Your work is important—so is mine, for that matter—but there is more to life than work."

"If it were just the two of us, I would probably risk it,"

she admitted, her hands still clenched in front of her. "If we tried and failed to make it work between us—because of our schedules, or whatever other obstacle might crop up—one or both of us might get hurt. I could deal with that. But I won't risk hurting Alice."

Her adamancy was beginning to shake his own optimism. Was he letting the pleasures of the past three weeks cloud his judgment about his daughter?

Alice was already paying the price of having a mother who was obsessed with her career. And no matter how hard he tried to prevent it, there were still times his own job interfered with things Alice wanted to do. Was it really fair to bring another workaholic into her life?

He still thought it was possible to make this work—though it would take an extraordinary amount of effort on everyone's part. If either of them wasn't willing to make that effort—whether for fear of hurting Alice or just due to doubt that it was all worth the trouble—they had no chance of success. That was the ultimate lesson he had learned from his failed marriage. And Meagan was making it pretty clear she wasn't that strongly invested.

"Maybe—" He sighed, pushing a hand through his drying hair. "Maybe I'd just better go. Sorry about the tea."

She glanced at the now-cooling mugs without interest.

He moved toward the doorway. Meagan remained where she stood.

One foot out of the room, he looked back at her. "Three weeks ago, you invited me over for a swim, even though I'd been kind of a jerk to you. My first thought was to say no, because I had convinced myself it wouldn't work without even giving us a chance. But you looked me in the eye, and you told me that if I changed my mind, the invitation stood."

He could still picture her standing there on his walkway,

her expression warm and unguarded as she had risked yet another rejection. "Well, I changed my mind. And I'm damned glad I did."

She didn't speak, merely looked at him, hands still locked, as was her expression.

Feeling like a proper idiot now, he shrugged. "All I'm saying is—if you change your mind, the invitation stands. To give it a try, I mean. Good night, Meagan."

He thought he should leave before he made an even bigger fool of himself.

Meagan didn't try to stop him.

Chapter Eleven

Twenty-four hours after Alice's return from Europe, she was still full of stories to share with Seth. She babbled almost endlessly, showed him what seemed like a million snapshots and souvenirs, demonstrated some of the foreign phrases and customs she had learned on her trip. She'd had a wonderful time, but she said she was very glad to be home.

"Waldo's grown like a foot!" she marveled, her arms wrapped tightly around the wiggling dog's neck Sunday afternoon. She'd beelined straight to the dog the moment she'd walked into the house yesterday, and had hardly left him since. Seth had begun to wonder only half-humorously if she'd missed Waldo as much as she had missed him. She had been playing with the dog again for the past hour, and Seth had just come out to join them. "Thank you, thank you, thank you for taking care of him for me, Dad."

Standing on the patio near the door, he smiled. "You're

welcome. You'll have to thank Jacqui tomorrow, too. She's had to take care of him during the days. She's worked with him quite a bit, too. Walked him on the leash to keep him in training. Kept him entertained during the daytimes so he wouldn't get too lonely for you."

"I will thank her." Taking the dog's grinning face between her hands, Alice dropped a kiss on top of his head. "I've got five whole weeks before school starts again, Waldo. We'll spend every day together now, I promise."

Waldo wagged his tail as if he understood and approved every word.

Straightening, she lifted her hair off her neck, her skin glistening with a sheen of perspiration after her strenuous play with her dog. "Wow. It's hot."

"Still in the nineties," he agreed, feeling the stifling, humid air pressing through his T-shirt and cargo shorts. "You've gotten used to that milder, European summer. Forgot what July can feel like in Arkansas. You've got two weeks to get used to it again before we get into the August inferno."

"That's what pools are for," she said, waving a hand expressively at their sizeable backyard.

He chuckled, amused by her persistence. "Next year."

Though they couldn't see it from the back yard, she glanced in the general direction of Meagan's house and he had little trouble following her line of thought. She'd asked about Meagan several times already since he'd met her at the airport the day before. He'd told her only that yes, he had seen Meagan a few times during the month Alice was gone, and that she was fine.

"I want to take Meagan the scarf I brought her from France. Is it okay if I call her now to see if she's home?"

"She said you're welcome to call any time. If she's busy,

she'll let the call go to voice mail and you can leave her a message asking when would be a good time."

"She's probably not working on a Sunday afternoon."

"She could be," he said with a shrug. "Trust me, Alice, she works a lot. When she's on call, she has to be prepared to rush to the hospital at any moment to do surgeries. When she's not at the hospital, she's often in meetings with her partners or professional organizations or spending time with her mother who is taking care of Meagan's very ill grandmother."

Yet with all those responsibilities, she had made time to be with him during the past month, he thought somberly. Which only showed that they could have worked things out, schedule-wise, had their relationship progressed the way he had begun to hope it would.

"Dad." Alice tucked a curl behind her ear, and not for the first time he thought that Waldo wasn't the only one who'd matured during the past month.

He'd noticed subtle changes in his little girl since she'd returned from her European adventures. He couldn't put a finger on what those changes were, exactly, but she seemed a little more self-possessed, a little less childish. She'd cut her hair again while she was gone, and he was still getting used to seeing her without her cute little round glasses. Her mother had bought her practically an entirely new wardrobe of age-appropriate but more fashionable clothes, but there was more to the transformation than outward appearance. Perhaps it was just a new confidence born out of traveling so far from home by herself.

"Dad," she repeated, snapping him out of his wistful musings.

"Sorry. What?"

"Did you and Meagan go out while I was gone? You know, on dates?"

He hesitated a moment before answering lightly, "We had dinner together a few times when neither of us had other plans. I think she was trying to keep me from being too lonely for you."

"You like her, don't you?"

"Of course I like her. She's a very nice person."

Alice frowned at him in censure for the prevarication. "You know what I mean. You *really* like her."

He shrugged and tried to change the subject. "What do you want for dinner tonight? I was thinking maybe we could go out, if you want. You'd probably like a good old American burger or Arkansas barbecue after all that fancy European food."

Alice refused to be sidetracked from her interrogation. "Are you going to have dinner with her again? Just the two of you, I mean. A date."

He sighed. "What did I tell you about matchmaking? Meagan and I are just friends, Alice."

"But you would be more, wouldn't you? If it weren't for me, I mean." Looking troubled, she rested a hand absently on Waldo's head when the dog pushed against her for more attention. "You don't have a personal life when I'm here because you think you have to be here all the time for me."

Scowling, he took a step toward her. "I spend time with you because I choose to, Alice. I don't consider it a sacrifice to be with my daughter. If your mother said anything to you—"

"She didn't," Alice assured him a little too quickly. "I mean, maybe I mentioned that we'd met Meagan and that you and Meagan seemed to hit it off—and maybe Mom said it's got to be tough for a single dad with a busy schedule to find time to date—but she wasn't criticizing. She said some really nice things about you, in fact. She said she's happy you're such a good father. She said she wishes she were more like you—you know, content to stay here in Arkansas and lead a settled sort of life with your daughter."

A settled sort of life. He could almost hear Colleen saying the words—and they weren't quite the compliment Alice took them to be.

"Your mom doesn't really know what's going on in my life," he said carefully, trying to keep any measure of censure from his tone. "I'm very happy to have you back home again. Don't ever doubt that."

"I don't. I just want you to know you don't have to spend every minute with me. I'm thirteen years old. I have a life, myself, you know. Tiff wants to have a sleepover party next weekend and I'm going to be pretty busy this week catching up with my swim team and telling all my friends about my trip and everything. I thought maybe I could have Casey over one evening? Her grandma would bring her. I want to show her all my pictures and souvenirs and stuff."

"Casey's welcome to come over. And you can spend the night at Tiff's as long as at least one of her parents will be there to supervise," he said automatically. "And don't worry about me, kiddo. I can entertain myself for a few hours when you have other plans. You don't have to take care of me, either," he added in an attempt at levity.

She didn't smile. "Mom said you might be worried that if you start seeing someone seriously, I'd get upset if it didn't work out. When I bought the scarf for Meagan, she warned me not to get too upset if you and Meagan were to get together and then break up or something because most relationships don't work out, anyway. Especially when both people have busy careers, like you and mom did, or you and Meagan do now. So if you're worried about that, don't, Dad. I mean, I wouldn't want you to get hurt or anything, but sometimes these things do work out, you know? Tiff's parents are still together, and they both have careers. Her mom owns a boutique and she's there like seven days a week, and her dad does something at a bank, I think."

"Alice—" It sounded to him as though his daughter and his ex-wife had done entirely too much talking about his personal life.

He didn't want to fuss at Alice, really, because it was only natural for her to talk about her life during the month she'd spent with her mom, but Colleen shouldn't have encouraged talk about things that were really none of her business, no matter how helpful she'd considered herself being. Had it made her feel less culpable about their failed marriage to predict that he wouldn't be able to sustain a relationship with anyone else, either?

He had no intention of letting his ex find out that his most recent attempt had crashed and burned, too. He would never let either Alice or Colleen know that the sting of this failure could stay with him for a while, making him very unlikely to try again anytime soon. He had allowed himself to fall too hard for Meagan. Let himself start believing in things he'd given up on a long time ago. And it had hurt to watch those renewed fantasies disintegrate around him, especially since he wasn't entirely sure what he'd done wrong this time. He should have just stuck to his resolve to date only rarely, and then on a strictly casual and temporary basis.

"Just saying, Dad."

"Thanks," he said wryly, "but let's just leave things as they are for now, shall we? You and Meagan can still be friends, when you both have time to get together, but that's something the two of you started before I even met her, remember? So go ahead and call her, if you want, to see if she's home. I've got a few emails to return and then we can go out to dinner whenever you're ready."

She sighed, but seemed to get the message that he didn't want to talk about this any more for now. He started to turn back toward the house, then paused. "Oh, and Alice? Do not mention anything along these lines to Meagan, got it? No hinting that she and I should go out or anything like that. Nothing you and your mother talked about concerning me and relationships. Just tell her about your trip and leave me out of it."

His daughter rolled her eyes and that was one gesture that hadn't changed in the least while she was away. "Geez, Dad, give me some credit, will you?"

"Just saying."

Shaking her head in response to his repetition of her, she turned away. "Go answer your email. I'll give Waldo some fresh water before I come in to call Meagan."

Hoping this topic was behind them now, though he wouldn't be surprised if it cropped up again occasionally, he went inside, leaving his daughter pouting behind him.

"Alice, this scarf is lovely. I'll treasure it—but you really didn't have to bring me anything from your trip."

The girl seemed pleased by Meagan's reaction to the gift. "I didn't spend a lot for it," she said with the art-less candor Meagan had come to expect from her. "But I thought it looked like something you'd like. I've seen you wear that color green before."

"It's one of my favorite colors," Meagan assured her, running the silky fabric through her fingers. "Thank you."

"Well, you've been so nice to us. Rescuing Waldo and helping us with Nina and helping us find Jacqui and all. I wanted to do something nice for you, too."

Touched, Meagan set the scarf aside and reached out to give the girl a quick hug. "This was a very nice gesture. I'll wear it proudly."

"I'm glad you like it."

Meagan motioned toward the little red netbook computer Alice had set on the table. "I can't wait to see all your pictures. I'm glad you brought them with you."

"Dad told me not to bore you with them, because I took a lot, but I'll show you my favorites and if you get bored, you can just say so."

Meagan held her smile firmly in place. "I'm sure I'll enjoy them."

They sat side by side at the table, the netbook arranged where both could see the little screen. Meagan had made herbal tea for them and set out some cookies for Alice to munch on while they caught up. Meagan made appropriately admiring noises over the snapshots passing on the screen at a medium speed. Most of the photos were quite good; Alice was a competent photographer for her age. Quite a few of the shots featured her mother.

Meagan couldn't help but study those pictures of Colleen a bit more closely than the European landmarks and countryside. She was a little taken aback at her first sight of Seth's ex-wife. She hadn't expected Colleen to be quite so striking.

Alice had gotten her brown eyes from her mother, but where Alice's were a warm mahogany, Colleen's were almost black. Slightly almond shaped—an impression likely enhanced by skillful makeup. Alice's curls came from Seth's side of the family; Colleen's hair was a luxurious mane of chestnut waves. Like Meagan herself, Colleen probably resorted to salons for the color but it looked quite natural and attractive. She was slender to the point of thinness, dressed in fashionable dark colors, and looked competent, intelligent and successful.

Though Alice had inherited a few of her father's features, Meagan saw signs in Colleen of the woman Alice would become once she'd left adolescent awkwardness behind. At least physically. Meagan didn't know exactly how much Alice resembled her mother in other ways.

Meagan had been home from her mom's house only fifteen minutes when Alice had called half an hour ago to ask if she could come over with the gift and her pictures. Looking forward to seeing the girl again, Meagan had agreed with pleasure. She wasn't surprised when Alice had shown up alone, nor had Meagan extended a specific invitation for Seth to accompany her. Not that she would have turned him away, of course.

"It looks like you had a wonderful time," she said after half an hour of admiring the slideshow. "You were probably reluctant to return home."

"I had a fantastic time, but I was ready to come back. I missed my dad and Waldo and my friends. I missed you, too," Alice added a little shyly.

"I missed you, too," Meagan assured her—and she was being honest, she assured herself. It was nice to see the girl's sweet smile again, to laugh with her and hear her cheery chatter. Those weeks alone with Seth had been blissful, but the days just hadn't seemed quite complete even to Meagan without having Alice there at some point.

"I was afraid my dad would be really lonely with me gone." Alice's tone was just a bit too casual as she reached out to close the lid on her computer. "I heard you and he had dinner a few times. I'm glad he had you to keep him company."

"He, um, told you that?"

"Well, I asked if he'd seen you and he said yes, a few times."

He wouldn't lie to his daughter, Meagan thought. But he wouldn't have told her the whole truth about those weeks, either, of course.

"Yes, we visited a few times when neither of us had other plans." There. That sounded quite friendly and casual. "Can I get you any more tea, Alice? Or something else? I have juice and soda."

"No, thank you, I've had plenty. Dad said I have to be home by six because we're going out for dinner."

"That will be nice."

"You could come with us."

Meagan doubted that Seth would have appreciated Alice extending the invitation without consulting him first—and she would bet that there had been no such consultation. "Thank you for asking, but no. I have a few things to do here this evening to prepare for work tomorrow."

"I understand that you have to work a lot, you know. You've got lives to save. That's really important."

Meagan wasn't sure what to say. "Um, yes. My job does require long hours, but I think it's important, too. And I love doing it."

"It's good to love what you do. It makes you happy, and when you're happy, the people who love you are happy."

Maybe this oblique conversation had little to do with Seth. Maybe Alice was referring to her mother, perhaps implicitly defending Colleen's choice to pursue her dreams so far from her only child. "That's right. I hope you'll love being an orthodontist—or whatever you ultimately choose to do—as much as I love being a surgeon, and your parents enjoy practicing law in their own fields."

"I just wanted to say that, you know, I don't have a problem with you working so much. It doesn't hurt my feelings or anything when you can't do something because you have to save someone's life. I just like seeing you when you have some time."

"Um, thank you, Alice. I enjoy seeing you, too. Maybe you'd like to come for a swim next Sunday afternoon? I should be here for a few hours then. Of course, you're free to use the pool whether I'm here or not, as long as there's someone with you. I don't want you to ever swim alone."

The look Alice gave her held exasperation, as if she wondered whether Meagan was being deliberately obtuse. Meagan could have told her it was no act. She wasn't at all sure what the girl was getting at.

Alice looked as though she wanted very much to say something else, but after what appeared to be a mental struggle, she sighed and picked up her computer. "Okay. I'd better go. But just so you'll know, I've got a very busy summer ahead, myself. You know, swim team and hanging out with my friends and stuff. Dad will probably be on his own quite a bit. Now that I'm old enough to have my own life and stuff, you know."

Well, it couldn't be more clear than that. Meagan had a feeling Seth would not be happy that Alice was still trying to push them together. She wasn't particularly comfortable with the girl's machinations, herself.

Pretending to still be oblivious to Alice's hints, Meagan walked her to the door where she thanked her again for the scarf and promised to see her again soon. Alice was shaking her head a little when she walked down the sidewalk toward her house and Meagan could almost see the girl thinking, "Grown-ups!"

Though she doubted Alice would appreciate the overprotective gesture, Meagan stood in the doorway watching until the girl was safely home. Only then did she go back inside her own house and close the door.

A few days later, Meagan returned home from work at almost ten o'clock at night. She'd been detained at the hospital by a procedure that had taken almost an hour longer than expected that afternoon. Almost before she'd finished with that patient, another patient had been rushed into an O.R. with a complication from surgery the day before. Meagan had to rush to scrub, making an almost superhuman attempt to save the crashing patient's life.

When she left the hospital after several hours of painstaking reconstruction, she still wasn't sure her efforts had been successful. She would not have been at all surprised if her patient did not survive the night. As much as she truly hated to admit it, there were times when all her training and skills simply weren't enough.

Hungry and bone weary, she braked for her driveway. It was raining hard, as it had been all day, and she had to peer through the thumping wipers to see the turn through the downpour. She glanced automatically across the street to a house where warm lights glowed through the storm. She could just see the blue flicker of a TV screen in one window. Perhaps Seth and Alice were watching together in the dry shelter of their cozy den. Seth enjoyed eating popcorn and watching movies on his big TV.

Meagan pictured him and Alice sitting on the sofa laughing at something silly on the screen and mentally inserted herself into the picture, snuggled up with them. The fleeting fantasy did nothing to lighten her mood as she dragged herself into her kitchen and opened the fridge to make a cold sandwich. She was much too tired to cook anything.

She missed him—them, she corrected herself quickly. She enjoyed being with them. But she didn't belong in that picture. Seth and Alice had been a tight unit long before Alice stumbled into Meagan's backyard. She wouldn't be the one to disrupt the dynamics of that cozy household, to risk bringing pain and disappointment into a little family that had already seen its share.

Even as that noble thought crossed her mind for at least

the dozenth time in as many hours, she wondered if all her posturing about protecting Alice was really just a smoke-screen. More and more, she was beginning to suspect that it wasn't only Alice she was trying to shield from pain and disappointment. Nor Seth.

It seemed that for all her confidence in the operating room, she was quite the coward when it came to risking her heart. For years, she'd used her training and then her practice as an excuse for not letting down her guard. Was she now using Alice?

A rumble of thunder rattled her windows, followed by another gust of rain. Setting her sandwich aside only half eaten, she wandered into her bedroom and lay fully clothed on top of the covers. She should probably call her mother before it got any later, check on her grandmother. She had a few reports to look through, some notes to dictate. But she was so darned tired. How could she possibly add anything more to her already frantic schedule? And if she tried and failed, how many people would she hurt? How deeply would she suffer, herself?

Closing her eyes, she turned her face into the pillow. If failure hurt any worse than this lonely ache, she wasn't at all sure she could survive it.

Scrubbed and gloved, Meagan was just preparing to begin a simple lap appy early the next afternoon when her phone rang. Draped and snoozing, the patient lay on the table surrounded by the surgical team waiting for Meagan to begin. A third year medical student shifted restlessly as he waited for directions and undoubtedly hoped he wouldn't embarrass himself or earn the surgeon's or resident's censure. Meagan could hear the resident already giving instructions, warning the student about breaking the field or other operating room transgressions.

Because she hadn't yet started, she took the call, just in case it was important. She didn't receive many calls on her personal phone during her working hours, since her friends and family didn't want to disrupt her schedule. She didn't want to descrub, so she had the floater nurse hold the phone to her ear while Meagan kept her sterile hands carefully elevated. "Hello?"

"Meagan?" The young voice was choked with tears, hardly recognizable. "It's Alice."

"Alice? What's wrong? What's happened?"

The room went quiet behind her when the chatting team heard the instinctive panic in Meagan's tone.

"It's—it's Waldo. He's—" The words broke with a sob.

Meagan felt her heart clench. If anything had happened to Alice's beloved pet...

"He's missing," Alice finally finished. "He got out of the fence again, and we can't find him. He's been gone for hours. Jacqui and Daddy are looking for him. They told me to wait here at home in case anyone called. But I—I hope I'm not interrupting you, but I just wanted you to know."

"Oh, sweetheart, I'm sorry. I wish I could come help look for him right now, but I'm just about to start an operation. I'll be there as soon as I can, okay?"

"It's okay," Alice said forlornly. "I know you can't come, but I just needed to tell you. What if we never find him? What if he got hit by a car or something? What if he's—he's—"

"I'm sure he'll be okay," Meagan said with an optimism she had to force. "Your dad will find him."

"I hope so. I'm sorry I disturbed you," she said again.

"No, honey, I'm glad you called. I'll be there when I can. If you hear anything in the meantime, send me a text, okay? I'll have someone read it to me. Waldo will be fine, Alice. Your dad will bring him home to you."

"Okay. Thanks, Meagan."

Gale, of course, was the only one who had the nerve to question Meagan when she joined the team at the table, moving into position at the patient's left side, near the shoulder. Gale and Meagan had worked together hundreds of times during the past few years, and had bonded over numerous procedures. Meagan considered the scrub tech one of her best friends among her coworkers.

"What was that about?"

"A young friend's dog has disappeared. She's very upset about it. She's home by herself and I think she just wanted reassurance from someone she trusts that everything will be okay. I hope I was telling the truth when I assured her it would be."

"What else could you say?" Gale asked with a shrug, positioning the monitor so Meagan could see it clearly while working through three tiny cuts in the patient's abdomen. A tiny camera held by the resident would be inserted through the umbilical port, and Meagan would focus on that monitor as she removed the diseased appendix using the camera images for guidance.

"This young friend wouldn't happen to belong to that single dad you've been seeing, would she?"

Wincing a little behind her paper mask, Meagan nodded without looking up from her patient as she prepared to make the first small incision. "Yes."

"Uh-huh."

Scalpel poised, Meagan frowned at the tech. "What does that mean?"

Gale's eyes crinkled with a smile. "You'll be a great stepmom."

"Uh—let's just concentrate on our work, okay?"

"Whatever you say, Doc."

Calling on her years of training and practice to push extraneous thoughts to the back of her mind, Meagan turned her attention on her patient. She couldn't think about Alice's distress now. She could only say a quick prayer that Seth would bring his daughter's pet safely home.

Almost two hours had passed by the time Meagan made it to Seth's front door. She'd finished the procedure successfully, and then had had her secretary cancel all her appointments for the remainder of the afternoon. Fortunately there had been nothing too pressing; she would have to scramble a bit tomorrow to make up for her abrupt departure but she could manage.

She felt the muggy early August heat envelop her as she pressed the doorbell. It was a miserably hot afternoon, almost a hundred in the shade. She hoped Waldo was somewhere safe and cool and that he had access to water. She couldn't bear the thought of the silly mutt suffering in this heat.

Alice answered the bell. Her face was red and splotchy, her eyes swollen from crying. She burrowed into Meagan's arms. "I just talked to Dad on the phone. They still haven't found Waldo. He's gone, Meagan. I just know he's hurt or… or…"

Resting her head on the girl's tumbled curls, Meagan hugged her tightly. "Don't imagine the worst, honey. Waldo's probably fine. Maybe someone found him and took him to the animal shelter."

"Jacqui's checked all the shelters already. She's going to all the closest veterinary clinics now. Daddy's driving up and down streets looking for any sign of Waldo. He's been looking for almost three hours."

Alice must have called Meagan not long after her

father had started the search. "How long has Waldo been missing?"

The girl sniffled and wiped her damp face with her sleeve. "About four hours, I think. Jacqui and I walked all over the neighborhood looking for him before I called Dad. I thought maybe he'd gone to your house again, but he wasn't there. It took Dad about half an hour to take care of things at work so he could come help. And then I called you because—"

She sniffed again. "Because I'd been sitting here by myself thinking of all the terrible things that could have happened to Waldo and I thought—I don't know, you just helped so much when Nina was hurt."

"I'm sorry it took me so long to get here. What can I do to help now?"

"I don't know, I—" Falling silent, Alice cocked her head. "Is that Dad's car?"

She threw open the door. "It is. He's here, do you think—is that Waldo with him?"

Looking over Alice's head, Meagan laid a hand on the girl's shoulder. "Yes. I see him, in the backseat."

"He found him!" Turning to hug Meagan again, Alice repeated happily, "He found him. Daddy found Waldo."

They both hurried to welcome the errant dog home.

Had it not been for Alice's stress and her own deep relief, Meagan might have been amused by the sight Seth made when he climbed out of his car. Though he had discarded his jacket and tie, he still wore a dress shirt and suit pants. Both were caked with mud, as were his once-nice leather shoes. There was mud in his hair, on his hands and on his face, along with a deep scratch down one cheek that had oozed blood into the caked-on dirt. Sweat had trickled down his cheeks, leaving tracks in the grimy splotches.

He didn't see her immediately. He was dragging the

equally-muddy dog out of his car and muttering steadily beneath his breath, probably words he would just as soon his daughter didn't hear. Meagan had never seen him looking so bedraggled or frazzled. There was no telling how he'd gotten in that condition, but she knew there was nothing he would not have done to bring his daughter's beloved pet home to her.

Her chest clenched once, and then slowly relaxed as her heart beat with a peaceful new rhythm. A new purpose.

"Heel, Waldo," Seth said, and his tone had the dog falling immediately into position at the end of his leash, ears drooping and tail tucked.

"Waldo." Alice fell onto her pet, oblivious of the mess as she hugged him and searched him frantically for injuries. Keeping a wary eye on Seth, the dog greeted Alice with tail wags and licks.

Only then did Seth spot Meagan, who'd held back a little so as not to interfere with the reunion. His eyes widened in surprise at seeing her there at only four in the afternoon. "Meagan? What are you—"

"I called her, Dad," Alice said, just a hint of defiance in her still-husky voice. "I just wanted her to know."

Meagan had her eyes on Seth's injured face, which Alice hadn't even seemed to notice yet. "What happened?"

He shrugged. "Stupid dog had wandered down to the construction site on Candle Street. No one was working there today, probably because of all the mud from yesterday. He wiggled through an opening in a chain-link fence and got his collar caught on a piece of metal. I don't know how long he'd been there when I found him. Don't even know what made me look there, exactly, it was just the only place I hadn't looked within several miles of here. I had a heck of a time getting him free. Had to lie down in the mud with him to reach his collar and he kept squirming, and then he jumped up when I freed him and knocked me facefirst into the broken part of the fence."

"Ouch. Come inside and I'll clean it and look at it."

A small, slightly battered car pulled into the driveway and Jacqui jumped out. "Thanks for calling to let me know you'd found him, Seth. Oh, would you look at this mess. You go on inside and get cleaned up, Seth. Alice and I will turn a hose on Waldo and then see what we can do about cleaning the inside of your car, won't we, Alice?"

Alice's glance at her father showed she didn't dare object, even had she wanted to.

Leaving the mess in Jacqui's capable hands, Seth and Meagan went through the garage so he wouldn't track mud anywhere but the kitchen. He shed his ruined shoes before entering the house. Meagan led him straight to the sink, where she moistened a paper towel and dabbed carefully at his face, keeping her focus on the scratch.

"It doesn't look too bad. You don't need stitches, though you'll have a bruise and some puffiness for a few days. Are you current on your tetanus boosters?"

"Had one a couple of years ago when I cut my hand on a piece of metal during a fishing trip with a friend."

She nodded. "That's current enough. You'll be fine."

"Thanks." He caught her hand and lowered it from his face. "I'll clean up in the shower. Did you rush straight over here when Alice called you?"

She couldn't quite meet his eyes when she turned to toss the dirty towel in the trash. "I was just starting surgery, so it took me a couple of hours to get away. I'd only been here a few minutes when you got here with Waldo."

"Alice shouldn't have called you at work. I don't know what she was thinking."

"She was upset and here by herself and she wanted

to hear a friend's voice," Meagan answered with a slight shrug. "I didn't mind."

"I'm sorry. I'll tell her not to disturb you at work again."

"You'll do no such thing." She stepped directly in front of him to hold his gaze with her own. "Any time Alice needs me, she can call me. I can't promise that I'll always be able to drop everything and run to her, but I can guarantee I'll get to her as quickly as I can. I think she understands that's the best I can do. Of the three of us, she seems to be the most sensible about certain subjects."

"I don't know what you mean by that."

She smiled, laying a hand against his dirty cheek. "I'll have her explain a few things to you later."

He caught her hand in his, lowering it but not releasing it. His eyes drilled into hers. "What are you telling me, Meagan?"

"Your marriage didn't end because you both had careers. It ended because you were wrong for each other."

He shook his head in bemusement. "That's what I told you."

"I know. It just took me a little while to hear it. And to believe it," she admitted. "I said I was protecting Alice— but I've come to realize that I was protecting myself. I was the one who got scared this time. Scared of hurting her. Of hurting you. Of being hurt, myself. And for the first time in my life, I let fear keep me from pursuing something I wanted very badly. To be a part of your life. Yours and Alice's."

He lifted her hand to his mouth, dropping a kiss in her palm. "We both want very much for you to be a part of our lives."

"I've missed you, Seth."

"I've missed you, too. So much I ached."

A lump formed in her throat in response to his candor. She swallowed and whispered, "So the invitation still stands?"

"It was always open," he replied simply. "We both know it won't be easy, but I think we just might have a good chance of making this work between us."

She smiled up at him. "As my mom always says, nothing worth having comes easily."

"I think I'm going to like your mom."

He lowered his head to kiss her, but drew back at the last moment. "I'm filthy."

She laughed and caught his muddy, scratched face in her hands. "I don't care."

Rising on tiptoe, she pressed her mouth to his.

"Hey, Dad, do you know where the— Oh." Alice giggled and backed rapidly out the kitchen door again. "Never mind."

She closed the door with a thud.

Seth grimaced. "She's going to take full credit for this, you know. We'll never hear the end of it."

"That's okay," Meagan assured him, tugging him back down to her. "I'd rather give Alice the credit than Waldo."

His laughter was smothered in their happy kiss.

Epilogue

Outside the windows of Seth's cozy den, a bitterly cold wind whipped through the bare branches of the surrounding trees. Early darkness had settled, plunging the neighborhood into deep shadows brightened by the white and multicolored Christmas lights decorating almost every house on the street.

Inside the den, a jumble of opened boxes and discarded paper and ribbon littered the floor beneath the gaily decorated tree in one corner. Snuggled next to Seth on the couch, Meagan surveyed the mess lazily. She'd get around to picking up in a little while, she thought contentedly.

It was late on Christmas day and the holidays had passed in a blur of frantic activity. Parties and school activities for Alice. Work and social obligations for Seth and Meagan. Family holiday gatherings. A brief visit from Seth's father, a trip to Heber Springs so Alice could spend some time with her mother's family, and Christmas Day luncheon with Meagan's mother and siblings.

Her grandmother had passed away in early November. Seth and Alice had been there for Meagan, comforting her in her sadness. Meagan's mom was getting past the worst of her own grief now so that she'd been able to enjoy Christmas with her family.

This was the first chance in several days that Meagan and Seth had been able to simply relax and be still, nothing pressing on them to do at the moment. During the past four months, they had learned to mesh their schedules for the most part to include time with each other and with Alice—though they had all gotten used to having the occasional plan disrupted by the buzz of a cell phone, either Meagan's or Seth's. As they had expected, it hadn't been easy. There had been some stress, a few arguments, plenty of compromises. But it had so been worth it all, Meagan thought with a smile, nuzzling her cheek against Seth's shoulder.

Alice had just bundled up and gone outside into the backyard with its strongly reinforced fencing. She'd said she was going to feed her dog and then see how he looked in the fancy new leather-and-brass-stud collar Meagan had bought the dog impulsively for Christmas. Alice had been delighted with the gesture, and said she was sure Waldo would love it. She'd just left the room when Seth spoke.

"Feels good just to sit still for a few minutes, doesn't it?" he asked, unwittingly echoing her thoughts.

Meagan released a happy sigh. "It does. But I should be heading home soon before that predicted sleet starts falling later."

"Stay here tonight."

She gave him a chiding look. "We've talked about this."

Convinced it set a bad example for Alice, Meagan had refused to sleep over with Seth when Alice was at home. He spent nights at her place during Alice's weekend visits with her grandparents or sleepovers with friends and he and Meagan had "date night" once a week when their schedules allowed, after which Seth returned home at a respectable hour.

Meagan doubted that Alice was entirely naive about the extent of her father's relationship with Meagan, but she still thought it best to be discreet. Seth agreed, reluctantly, which made it rather a surprise that he'd suggested she stay tonight.

"You can bunk in the guest room and we'll all have breakfast together tomorrow," he said.

"Oh. I suppose I could do that. Since the weather's so nasty." It wasn't something she'd done before, both because she lived so close and because she wasn't entirely sure she trusted either Seth or herself not to sneak down the hall in the middle of the night.

"There's still one more gift I want to give you," Seth said, twisting on the couch to face her more fully.

She lifted her eyebrows. "You've already given me several nice gifts."

Nodding, he reached into his pocket. "This one's a little different."

Her heart thudded in her chest when he drew out a small velvet box. Holding her gaze with his, he opened it to reveal the glittering ring inside. "I don't like watching you go to your house across the street every night. I think it would be a lot easier for all of us if we combine our households into one."

She swallowed hard. "You're asking me to marry you because it makes it easier to arrange our schedules?" she asked, amused by the tack he had taken.

"I'm asking you to marry me because I love you and I want to spend the rest of my life with you," he replied evenly. "Easier scheduling is simply a side benefit."

They hadn't rushed into this, she thought, lowering her misty gaze to the beautiful ring he had chosen for her. They had taken every precaution to protect Alice and themselves from disappointment. There were still details they had to work out between them, still complications that could arise—but there came a point when they simply had to take a chance. To trust that the love they shared would be strong enough to smooth the inevitable difficulties.

Drawing a deep breath, she took that leap of faith. "I love you, too, Seth. And yes, I will marry you."

His face lightened with one of his beautiful smiles—surely he hadn't been in any doubt of what her answer would be? He drew her into his arms for a kiss of celebration.

Neither of them heard the excited giggle from the open doorway to the room. Peeking around the corner at the couple entwined on the couch, Alice pumped her fist and then gazed down smugly at the yellow dog grinning back up at her. His new collar gleamed smartly around his neck.

"We'll show them how you look in your new collar later, Waldo," Alice whispered, tugging him toward the kitchen. "They're very busy right now."

Her steps bouncing with satisfaction at a job well done, she led her pet away.

* * * * *

 **COMING NEXT MONTH**

Available January 25, 2011

SPECIAL EDITION

SSECNM0111

REQUEST YOUR FREE BOOKS!

2 FREE NOVELS PLUS 2 FREE GIFTS!

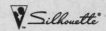

SPECIAL EDITION
Life, Love and Family!

YES! Please send me 2 FREE Silhouette® Special Edition® novels and my 2 FREE gifts (gifts are worth about $10). After receiving them, if I don't wish to receive any more books, I can return the shipping statement marked "cancel." If I don't cancel, I will receive 6 brand-new novels every month and be billed just $4.24 per book in the U.S. or $4.99 per book in Canada. That's a saving of 15% off the cover price! It's quite a bargain! Shipping and handling is just 50¢ per book.* I understand that accepting the 2 free books and gifts places me under no obligation to buy anything. I can always return a shipment and cancel at any time. Even if I never buy another book from Silhouette, the two free books and gifts are mine to keep forever.

235/335 SDN E5RG

Name	(PLEASE PRINT)	
Address		Apt. #
City	State/Prov.	Zip/Postal Code

Signature (if under 18, a parent or guardian must sign)

Mail to the Silhouette Reader Service:
IN U.S.A.: P.O. Box 1867, Buffalo, NY 14240-1867
IN CANADA: P.O. Box 609, Fort Erie, Ontario L2A 5X3

Not valid for current subscribers to Silhouette Special Edition books.

Want to try two free books from another line?
Call 1-800-873-8635 or visit www.morefreebooks.com.

* Terms and prices subject to change without notice. Prices do not include applicable taxes. N.Y. residents add applicable sales tax. Canadian residents will be charged applicable provincial taxes and GST. Offer not valid in Quebec. This offer is limited to one order per household. All orders subject to approval. Credit or debit balances in a customer's account(s) may be offset by any other outstanding balance owed by or to the customer. Please allow 4 to 6 weeks for delivery. Offer available while quantities last.

Your Privacy: Silhouette is committed to protecting your privacy. Our Privacy Policy is available online at www.eHarlequin.com or upon request from the Reader Service. From time to time we make our lists of customers available to reputable third parties who may have a product or service of interest to you. If you would prefer we not share your name and address, please check here. ☐

Help us get it right—We strive for accurate, respectful and relevant communications. To clarify or modify your communication preferences, visit us at www.ReaderService.com/consumerschoice.

HARLEQUIN®

A Romance

FOR EVERY MOOD™

Spotlight on

Classic

Quintessential, modern love stories that are romance at its finest.

See the next page
to enjoy a sneak peek from
the Harlequin® Romance series.

*Harlequin Romance author Donna Alward is loved
for her gorgeous rancher heroes.*

*Meet Wyatt as he's confronted by both a precious
little pink bundle left on his doorstep and his neighbor Elli
who's going to show him the ropes....*

Introducing
PROUD RANCHER, PRECIOUS BUNDLE

THE SQUAWKING QUIETED as Elli picked the baby up, and
Wyatt turned around, trying hard to ignore the feelings of
inadequacy as Darcy immediately stopped fussing.

"Maybe she's uncomfortable. What do you think, sweetheart?" Elli turned her conversation to the baby.

"What do you think is wrong?" Wyatt asked, putting the
coffee pot back on the burner.

A strange look passed over Elli's face, one that looked
like guilt and panic. But it was gone quickly. "I couldn't
say," she replied.

"But you were so good with her this afternoon." Wyatt
put his hands on his hips.

"Lucky, that's all. I just…remembered a few things."
The same strange look flitted over her features once more.

Wyatt took the coffee to the table. "You fooled me. You
looked like you knew exactly what you were doing." So
much so that Wyatt had felt completely inept. A feeling he
despised. He was used to being the one in control.

Elli and Darcy walked the length of the kitchen and
back. After a few moments, she admitted, "I haven't really
cared for a baby before. The things I thought of were simply
things I'd heard about. Not from experience, Mr. Black."

Her chin jutted up, closing the subject but making him

HREXP0211

want to ask the questions now pulsing through his mind. But then he remembered the old saying—*Don't look a gift horse in the mouth.* He'd benefit from whatever insight she had and be glad of it.

"I don't really know what babies need," he said. "I fed her, patted her back like you did, walked her to sleep, but every time I put her down…"

Wyatt almost groaned. Of course. He'd forgotten one important thing. He'd been so focused on getting the formula the right temperature that he'd forgotten to check her diaper. Not that he had any clue what to do there either.

Pulling calves and shoveling out stalls was far less intimidating than one tiny newborn.

"She's probably due for a diaper change, isn't she." He tried to sound nonchalant. This was a perfect opportunity. Elli must know how to change a diaper. He could simply watch her so he'd know better for the next time.

Instead, Elli came around the corner of the counter and placed Darcy back in his arms. "Here you go, Uncle Wyatt," she said lightly. "You get diaper duty. I'll fix the coffee. Cream and sugar?"

Oh boy, Wyatt thought, looking down into Darcy's pursed face, his smug plan blown to smithereens. He was in for it now.

Will sparks fly between Elli and Wyatt?

Find out in
PROUD RANCHER, PRECIOUS BUNDLE
Available February 2011 from Harlequin Romance

Try these Healthy and Delicious Spring Rolls!

INGREDIENTS

2 packages rice-paper spring roll wrappers (20 wrappers)

1 cup grated carrot

¼ cup bean sprouts

1 cucumber, julienned

1 red bell pepper, without stem and seeds, julienned

4 green onions finely chopped— use only the green part

DIRECTIONS

1. Soak one rice-paper wrapper in a large bowl of hot water until softened.

2. Place a pinch each of carrots, sprouts, cucumber, bell pepper and green onion on the wrapper toward the bottom third of the rice paper.

3. Fold ends in and roll tightly to enclose filling.

4. Repeat with remaining wrappers. Chill before serving.

Find this and many more delectable recipes including the perfect dipping sauce in

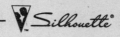

SPECIAL EDITION

FROM *USA TODAY* BESTSELLING AUTHOR

CHRISTINE RIMMER

COMES AN ALL-NEW BRAVO FAMILY TIES STORY.

Donovan McRae has experienced
the greatest loss a man can face, and
while he can't forgive himself, life—
and Abilene Bravo's love—are still
waiting for him. Can he find it in himself
to reach out and claim them?

Look for

DONOVAN'S CHILD

available February 2011